A Practical Joke?

Suddenly Dooley dropped into a crouching position and wheeled around facing the class. To my astonishment, I saw there was a gun in his hand.

"I guess I'm going to have to blow you guys away," Dooley said. His black eyes narrowed and he smiled.

Suzanne Yelverton began sobbing in big whooping noises. Dooley spun around to face her. "And I'm going to start with you," he growled.

Suzanne's eyes rolled up to show the whites and she slumped in her desk.

"Good grief," said Dooley in disgust. "Can you believe that? She's fainted."

Behind me, I heard soft thuds as the kids hit the deck. I would have tried to take cover, too, if my legs hadn't been limp.

Suddenly Dooley squeezed the trigger. A stream of water hit Suzanne square in the face.

Books by Janice Harrell

Andie and the Boys
Doolie Mackenzie Is Totally Weird
Easy Answers
Senior Year at Last
Wild Times at West Mount High

Available from ARCHWAY Paperbacks

Dooley Mackenzie

IS TOTALLY WEIRD

Janice Harrell

AN ARCHWAY PAPERBACK
Published by POCKET BOOKS

New York   London   Toronto   Sydney   Tokyo   Singapore

This book is a work of fiction. Names, characters, places and incidents are either the product of the author's imagination or are used fictitiously. Any resemblance to actual events or locales or persons, living or dead, is entirely coincidental.

AN ARCHWAY PAPERBACK *Original*

An Archway Paperback published by
POCKET BOOKS, a division of Simon & Schuster
1230 Avenue of the Americas, New York, NY 10020

ISBN: 0-671-69669-6

First Archway Paperback printing February 1991

10 9 8 7 6 5 4 3 2 1

AN ARCHWAY PAPERBACK and colophon
are registered trademarks of Simon & Schuster.

Printed in the U.S.A.

Cover photo by Mort Engel

IL 6+

Dooley Mackenzie

IS TOTALLY
WEIRD

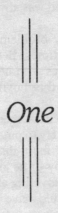

One

"I *need* a boyfriend," I told Chris Hamilton as I shifted my books to my other hip. "I've got to have one."

Astonished, he turned his blue eyes on me. "Where'd you get a crazy idea like that?"

Chris had the kind of blazing good looks that drew the opposite sex like an electromagnet, so I didn't really expect him to understand how desperate I was.

I tried to explain patiently. "You've heard of Noah's ark, where the animals went in two by two? Since then it's a well-known fact that two is the basic number. Besides, now that P.J. is all tied up with Susie Skinner, I need another way to go places. I need *wheels.*"

P.J. was my stepbrother. Since I couldn't get a North Carolina driver's license until I had finished a semester of driver's ed., he was supposed to drive me anywhere I needed to go. But lately he had commandeered our Camaro and was always off in it with Susie Skinner.

"If that's your only problem," Chris said, "I can give you a ride sometimes. Besides what about Rachel? You can go places with her. Believe me, Andie, you'd better rethink this boyfriend stuff. You'll be making a big mistake."

Considering the circumstances, I thought it was in poor taste for Chris to try to put me off romance. After all, it was partly his fault that I was having such trouble attracting a boy. If he and Dooley Mackenzie and P.J. hadn't been hovering around me like permanent chaperons, I would have had something going before now.

"I don't know how you can stand there and lecture me," I said. "You've got girls all over the place."

"Sure, I've got girls, but it isn't the same as having *a* girl. It's the difference between going out with somebody and going together."

"I don't follow you."

"Think about it. I go out and have a good time and that's one thing, but if a girl starts acting like she owns me, that's something else. *Now* do you follow me?"

"You know something, Chris? I think you've got a little problem with commitment."

"I don't have any problems with girlfriends, though." He grinned.

The bell rang over our heads with a nerve-shattering jangle just then, and I joined the crush of people filing toward the auditorium. It was the day for assembly, and I felt as if I were getting sucked into the auditorium against my will. Bodies and notebooks were pressed against me on every side. Somehow I eventually found myself at the section of seats assigned to my homeroom and fell into a seat next to the aisle.

Beside me sat a blond girl with stringy hair. She blew a bubble, then sucked the gum neatly back into her mouth. "Say, do you know Chris Hamilton?"

"Sort of," I admitted. "He's a good friend of my stepbrother's."

"Neat! I saw you with him a minute ago, so I figured you must know him."

I opened my French book and pretended to be studying. I hated conversations where perfect strangers tried to pump me about what Chris likes in a girl. The only honest answer would have been "a fast turnover."

"J'aime, tu aimes, il aime," I repeated softly to myself. I love; you love; he, she, or it loves. The moral of my French grammar was clear. Everybody loves. Why not me? Chris must be out of his mind if he believed I was going to take romantic advice from him. A list of the girls he had dated looked like something put out by the Census Bureau. Even if I had been able to attract boys on that scale, I wasn't up to such a fast-paced love life. I'd be sure to get the guys mixed up, and the first thing I knew, I'd call my current one by the name of my previous sweetie.

No, I had my own ideas about romance. I figured I needed one steady, secure love object—to be specific, Pete Joyner. When I first met Pete, I had been intimidated by him because his neck was the size of most people's thighs and because he always took a moment to consider the tensile strength of a chair before he sat on it. He was big. I think I had some fear that he would step on my toes and flatten them. But when we were working on a history project, I got to know him and discovered how sweet he was. Equally important, he seemed to be very interested in me. Since I was new at the game of attracting boys, I felt it would be smart to begin with someone who was already softened up.

The auditorium was packed now. Behind me someone yelped, "Ouch!" Another poor sucker had been hit by a flying battery. Lately kids had been taking the batteries out of their calculators and throwing them at unsuspecting classmates. It had been going on for weeks. Even though the student handbook had ten pages of fine print on what we couldn't do, it didn't stop the crazy battery war.

P.J. sat down across the aisle from me. His friend Dooley MacKenzie was with him. P.J., Dooley, and Chris were together pretty much all the time, like the Three Musketeers. I had noticed, though, that when one of them got interested in a girl, he tended to drop out of the gang for a while. Girls didn't want to tag along with three guys, which was no surprise. I wouldn't have tagged along with them myself if I had any choice. Half the time I had to catch a ride with them someplace, and the other half of the time I couldn't avoid them because they were at our house raiding the refrigerator. Out of necessity I had become an unofficial part of their gang.

When the band began playing "The Star-Spangled Banner," we shuffled to our feet. It was a minute or two before I realized something was wrong.

"That doesn't sound like 'The Star-Spangled Banner' to me," I whispered to the girl with stringy hair.

She didn't hear me because she was chanting softly with the music, "Jer-emiah was a bullfrog . . ." It

4

dawned on me then that what the band was playing was the funky bullfrog song I had sung at camp when I was little. I glanced over at the band and saw that the piccolos and the flutes were looking at one another in confusion. Laughter trickled through the auditorium. The band knew they were playing the wrong thing, and one by one they faltered and stopped playing— except for the tuba. Then somebody must have kicked him because he stopped too. All of us stood for a second longer, wondering what to do. Finally we began sitting down, and the auditorium buzzed with our whispers.

Mr. Vinson, the band director, hurriedly bent over to consult with the band members. Kids were waving music at him. Little wisps of Mr. Vinson's thin hair were standing on end. Band members groped for their music, and a flute stand clattered to the floor. Mr. Vinson lifted his hand, and with a bold blast of the horns the band struck up the school's alma mater. I had to give them credit. They played almost as if nothing had happened.

That was when I noticed P.J. nudging Dooley and grinning. Dooley's face had darkened into a guilty blush.

"Dooley!" I exclaimed. "It was Dooley!"

"What did you say?" asked the girl next to me. "Come again?"

"Shh!" A teacher frowned at us.

"What?" the girl insisted. But with my homeroom teacher looking at me, I didn't dare say anything. Maybe it was just as well. Even if Dooley *had* switched the music, the last thing I wanted to do was get him in trouble.

Mr. Hawkins, the principal, came out to the microphone and grabbed it with both hands as if he were going to eat it. It didn't take a subtle understanding of body language to see that he was mad. "I want to make it perfectly plain, people," he snarled, "that I will not allow the lawless minority to interfere with the rights of those students who are here to get an education." His voice sounded hollow over the loudspeaker system. "Is that understood? Practical jokes, vandalism, hooliganism of any kind will be dealt with promptly and forcefully. Did you hear me? *Forcefully.*" A ringing noise from the mike interrupted him. He scowled until it stopped. "Accordingly, as of tomorrow, any transistor radios or calculators found on campus will be confiscated at once." A collective groan swept over the auditorium. "There will be no exceptions," he snapped. "Math morons will just have to cope. I trust I have made myself clear."

"Yes, Your Majesty," someone behind me muttered.

"There may be more of you people than there are of us," continued Mr. Hawkins, sounding faintly hysterical now, "but we are the ones in charge. Do you understand? *We* are in charge!" He hurried off the stage and into the wings.

A battery missed my ear and fell into my lap. It lay there winking in the dim light, a small round battery like the ones used in cameras. I twitched my knees and flipped it to the floor. I didn't want to be caught with it on me. It was obvious that Mr. Hawkins was getting all geared up to make an example of somebody. He was definitely sounding paranoid. I mean, what had happened to his "partners in education" he had been giving us at the beginning of the year?

The student body president, a pink-faced blond kid

with a phony smile, came to the microphone. "And now," he said, "for our presentation on drugs—'Four Ways to Fry Your Brain.'"

A slide flashed on the screen behind him and I promptly shut my eyes. If people are going to do awful things to their noses, I'd rather not know about it. Besides, I had more pressing matters on my mind. Like Pete Joyner. I was sure he was interested in me. Absolutely positive. In American history I had felt his eyes following me when I got up to go to the pencil sharpener. And six times in the past two weeks he had "accidentally" bumped into me in the halls. But he hadn't gotten to the point of asking me out yet. If this kept up much longer, I was going to have to fall back on the well-known effects of green M&M's. I had known people who swore by them. This is the way it works. You eat all the red M&M's out of a bowl at a party and leave the bowl right in front of the object of your affections. Said object scoops up a handful of M&M's, all green, stuffs them in his mouth, and *pow,* he's done for. Green M&M's work like a love potion. The only problem was that the bags with only reds and greens are pretty hard to come by until Christmastime, and I wasn't sure I could wait that long. Some other girl might have gotten to Pete by then.

Luckily, I did have other options. After assembly, instead of going straight to my first-period class, I made a quick detour by the candy machine. I knew that because Pete was so big he needed frequent infusions of peanuts and chocolate to keep from feeling faint with hunger, and he stopped by the candy machines often. My plan was to run into him and stun him with my charm and bold wit. There wasn't much time for charm and wit when we met in the halls. There, exchanging any words more complicated than *hi* put us at risk of getting trampled.

"Andie!" Pete's deep voice boomed behind me.

I turned and saw him grinning broadly at me. Bingo! So far, so good. His brown eyes were soft, kind, melting. Looking into them, my knees turned to jelly. I searched desperately for something to say.

"Can you believe that junk about confiscating the transistors and the calculators?" I gulped. "I mean, did you hear Mr. Hawkins? I think he's finally snapped. Any minute I expected him to call for the firing squad. No kidding."

Pete grinned. "He was mad, all right. It was that 'Star-Spangled Banner' stuff that did it. Hawkins is a veteran. Messing up 'The Star-Spangled Banner' is the kind of thing that's bound to trip his switch."

Remembering Dooley's guilty look at the time of the crime, I could feel my shoulders scrunching up with anxiety. Suddenly I regretted bringing up the matter of "The Star-Spangled Banner." I'm no good when it comes to hiding things.

"Toni Andress told me somebody changed the middle page of the band's music," Pete went on. "Do you know Toni? She plays first clarinet."

What was Pete doing having cozy chats with Toni Andress? He was supposed to be interested in me! "Did Toni think"—I looked at him cautiously— "that somebody did it on purpose?"

"Sure, it was on purpose. What else? The thing is, the band doesn't play that bullfrog song at all. They'd never even seen the music before, so it wasn't like an ordinary mix-up. Nobody can figure out how that music got in there. But the band room was open, so I guess just about anybody could have done it if they'd wanted to."

I didn't want to be the one to bring up Dooley's name. After all, I told myself, I couldn't be absolutely sure that my suspicions were on target.

"I heard some kids say that Craig Bennett and his bunch were behind it," said Pete.

"That must be it," I agreed at once.

"You know Craig?"

"No. But I can't think who else it could be. Can you?" My eyes searched his face.

"Not a clue. Whoever it was, they're out of their mind. Catch me doing something like that! Sure, it was funny and all that, but it's the kind of thing that can end up on your permanent record."

"If you get caught."

"Yeah, but look at it this way," said Pete, dropping some coins in the candy machine. "How hard is it going to be to find out who bought all those copies of the bullfrog song?" The candy fell out of the machine with a thud.

He was right! But surely Dooley couldn't have been so stupid as to buy the music downtown. I knew he was no great brain, but I credited him with an instinct for basic self-preservation, at least.

"Say, how'd you like to go to that thing they're having at the playhouse this weekend?" Pete asked me. *The Actor and the Assassin,* it's called. It's supposed to be a gripping drama."

"I simply adore gripping dramas." I smiled at him.

"Me too." He looked relieved. "I'll pick you up early and we'll get some dinner first."

"Great—that sounds great," I said. Okay, it wasn't exactly sparkling repartee. But he must like me. He had asked me out, hadn't he?

Pete stuck half a PayDay into his mouth, struggled to smile, failed, then ambled off.

Jubilant, I sagged against the brick wall of the candy machine alcove. The bell for first period went off over my head, sounding like a celebration. Pete's and my relationship had passed an important mark. No more working together on history projects. No more brief exchanges of glances by the pencil sharpener. He had asked me out on an actual date. And not just a movie either. Dinner and the theater! We were talking major financial commitment here. My heart was pounding with excitement as I dashed off to class.

In American history class, I managed to pass a note to my friend Rachel Green.

"Don't look around now," I wrote, "but Pete's asked me to go to a play this weekend. Is that fantastic, or what?"

Rachel returned my note with her barely decipherable scrawl at the bottom. I think it said, "Zowie! Congrats!" It might have said "Zaire! Cougars!" but that seemed distinctly less likely.

I was so thrilled about my date with Pete that all the stuff about Dooley and "The Star-Spangled Banner" went completely out of my mind.

After school Dooley, P.J., and Chris Hamilton sat around our kitchen scarfing down food in alarming quantities. As I watched them I found myself wondering about the capacity of the human stomach. In diagrams of internal organs the stomach appeared to be quite small. Yet those three guys stuffed quantities of food into it that would have sustained whole villages. I decided that their stomachs must stretch. That was the only possible explanation.

Chris bit into a vast submarine sandwich. I was only a few yards away in the family room, my French book open on my lap, trying to concentrate on my work. Occasionally I got distracted by the rustle of paper, a quiet burp, and scraps of conversation.

"Geez, that assembly this morning. What a riot!" The fridge door closed and there was a moment of silence. P.J. was assembling his sandwich. "Could you believe the way Biff Henderson kept sitting there going *ooom-pah, ooom-pah* on that stupid tuba? Unreal."

"The building could come down around that turkey's ears and he wouldn't notice," Chris said. "I'm just glad I didn't miss the whole thing. This was no day to skip school. It was too priceless to miss. How'd you do it, Dooley?"

"Easy," Dooley croaked. "They don't lock up the music room. I just got forty copies of the bullfrog music down at the music store and switched the inside pages."

"The *local* music store?" I put in.

"Yeah, why?"

"I just wondered."

"Their faces! It was great." Chris grinned. "I wish I'd thought of it. How'd you get the idea?"

"Dunno. It just came to me." Dooley snapped his fingers.

"It was a classic." P.J. shook his head. "To tell you the truth, Dooley, old boy, I didn't know you had it in you."

I studied Dooley closely, trying to read his mind,

11

but it was hopeless. I never could read any of the guys' minds. In some basic way they were mysteries to me. I think it was because until my mom married Richard, P.J.'s dad, I didn't really know any boys all that well. I had lived in a more or less female universe where all the people I was truly close to were interested in such questions as whether it was best to shave or wax one's legs. It was very possible that I had not completely adjusted to living surrounded by males.

Whenever I saw the guys pigging out around the kitchen counter, I wanted to ask, "What's wrong with this picture?" They were such completely different types. Dooley had olive skin and heavy-lidded black eyes. He was a nice person, but there was no denying he looked like a character from *The Godfather, Part II*, while P.J., with his skinny legs and cowlick, looked more like a paperboy from a Norman Rockwell calendar. If P.J. had been the one to pull the trick on the band, I would have been able to understand. It was his kind of thing. He liked fire drills, wild parties, dogs chasing cats. He was just plain into commotion, but Dooley wasn't like that. Dooley was a quiet, basically gentle soul. And then there was Chris, who had glamour enough for all three of them. Tall, blond, and good-looking, all he had to do was zap girls with his industrial-strength come-hither look, and they lost all reason. I was sure this was bad for his character, but I had to admit that I wouldn't have minded having his knack for attracting the opposite sex.

The weird thing was that as different as the three guys appeared on the outside, they thought alike. To them the all-time dream job was sports broadcaster, the best movie featured plenty of blood, and the most fun thing they could do on a weekend was go to a big party that ended with somebody calling the police. They were very different from me. They were also a bit overwhelming.

With three of them and only one of me, it could be tricky to maintain my own point of view. One morning I woke up in a cold sweat after dreaming that I actually liked football.

Ever since Mom had married Richard and we moved into his large, ranch-style house, I had lived with track shoes, lacrosse shoes, copies of *Sports Illustrated,* and empty packages of Doritos that had been carelessly tossed aside. Inevitably there were socks under every sofa. A house-cleaning service that came in twice a week wasn't enough to wipe out the flavor of the locker room P.J. and his friends gave the place.

Down in the garage, below the house, P.J. had every sort of weird bodybuilding equipment—wheels to stretch himself on and treadmill devices to exhaust himself on, and a rowing machine designed to simulate conditions experienced by the galley slave. To anyone unfamiliar with the physical fitness craze, the garage would have looked like a torture chamber. They wouldn't have been far wrong.

I liked all three of the guys. I even felt a certain loyalty to them. But I needed a life of my own, a life away from them. I had considered the usual alternatives—leaving home to join a nunnery, pleading with my mom to let me go away to an all-girls' school, getting my own apartment in the city while I supported myself by doing macramé. But all of these options had massive drawbacks. The more I thought about it, the more I realized that I didn't need to get rid of the guys. All I needed was to get myself a boyfriend.

I knew that there was all the difference in the world between a romantic relationship and a friend-type boy-girl relationship. It seemed clear that when a boy was your boyfriend you had him on your own terms. I had witnessed it since P.J. had fallen for Susie Skinner. As soon as he started going out with her, he began shaving the stubble on his upper lip. Also, he showered frequently and always smelled strongly of Old Leather. He smiled a lot in a kind of self-conscious way when Susie was around, and I had once even seen him open a door for her. It was quite a shock. If P.J. or any one of the guys had opened a door for me, I would have figured the house was on fire. In my presence they were all, as you might say, completely natural and unretouched. They belched. They walked on their hands. They also had a way of butting into my business just when I wanted them to get lost.

I was sure there had to be more to life than being their mascot. I wanted to be treasured, adored, the whole nine yards. I wanted that worship-the-ground-you-walk-on stuff. And with Pete Joyner, I figured, I had the perfect opportunity. The gang might scare off other guys who were interested in me, but they wouldn't mess with Pete. In fact, it was sort of the other way around. When he looked at them, they tended to fidget and fade away.

As I stared down at my book, I could hear the clatter of dishes and the sound of running water in the kitchen. "Come back tonight," P.J. was saying. "And we'll work out." There was a scraping of chairs on the floor and grunts that I guess meant okay as Chris and Dooley departed.

"What's the matter with Dooley?" I asked P.J. after they left. "That stuff he did with the music this morning made Mr. Hawkins awfully mad."

P.J. snorted. "You aren't afraid of dumb old Hawkins, are you?"

Actually, I was. That was only one of the many ways in which I was different from the guys.

"But what if Dooley gets caught?" I said.

"He's not going to get caught. What are you giving me, Andie? You telling me he's not supposed to have any fun? Is that it?"

"I'm not saying that!" I hesitated. "But, honestly, P.J., weren't you pretty surprised when you found out he'd done it?"

P.J. smiled. "Yeah. This time, ol' Dooley outdid himself, all right."

"No, but really. Think about how much trouble it had to be to do all that stuff. I mean, he doesn't hand in half his algebra homework, but suddenly he has the time and the motivation to do this. Why?"

"Aw, come on, Andie!"

"Don't you worry about him?"

"Not when it comes to this kind of thing." P.J. turned and stomped upstairs, looking thoroughly disgusted. My stepbrother might resemble someone painted by Norman Rockwell, but his disposition was strictly out of the Addams Family.

Maybe it didn't make sense for me to worry about Dooley. It was possible that I suffered from a "Wendy" complex—you know, the compulsion to look after the Lost Boys and mend their socks. But I couldn't help it. I couldn't stop thinking of how awful it would be if Dooley got caught. He might get expelled!

Dooley didn't really have anybody to look after him. His mother had joined some weird cult when he was little, and his father had a job that kept him traveling during the week. So for all practical purposes, Dooley was an orphan. He did his own cooking and kept house by a method that involved washing the dishes once a week and sort of hosing down the house now and then. I kept wanting to ply him with fresh vegetables and vitamin pills, but my friend Rachel insisted that he was getting along fine. In fact, according to her, he liked everything just the way it was.

Rachel, who lives next door to me, is my best friend. In spite of this, she always takes the guys' side whenever I complain about them. I guess I understand it. I don't like it, but I understand it. Naturally, she wasn't going to have the same attitude toward them as I did. I had to regularly elbow them aside to get to the refrigerator. Also, at one time she had had a huge crush on Chris. She'd gotten over it, but I had reason to think she was getting a thing about Dooley now. So she wasn't exactly impartial.

Rachel has black hair that reaches to her shoulder blades, violet blue eyes, long skinny legs, and a mind like a steel trap. I was eager to get her opinion of Dooley's "Star-Spangled Banner" caper. But since I knew she was grounded and not allowed any visitors, I took my French book when I went next door.

Rachel's mother looked at me suspiciously when she answered the door. "French test Friday," I said brightly. I don't know if Mrs. Green actually believed me, but she didn't stop me from going upstairs to Rachel's room.

Rachel's house looked as if it had been built by a Chinese who got rich in the laundry business. It was spotless. Not a dust mote marred the marble expanses and T'ang dynasty reproductions. The Oriental rugs always showed fresh carpet sweeper marks. There were pale green walls and lighted alcoves everywhere filled with big Chinese vases.

Rachel's room was another story. That was where interior decoration ended and mess began. I suppose there was a rug in there, but I couldn't have sworn to it. The floor was always covered with books, papers, and magazines. Mrs. Green coped by never entering her daughter's room. Very possibly, now that I thought of it, that was what Rachel had in mind.

I closed the door to her room behind me and carelessly tossed my book on the floor. It slid to a stop on a pile of papers. "It was Dooley who slaughtered 'The Star-Spangled Banner' this morning," I said.

"No kidding!" Rachel's eyes widened. "How'd he do it?"

"Doesn't anybody but me see the gravity of this situation?" I scooped some clothes off Rachel's bed and sat down.

"Oh, come on, Andie, lighten up. What does it matter? Nobody can sing 'The Star-Spangled Banner' anyway. Who cares whether they play it right or not? I thought the whole thing was pretty funny. Didn't you?"

"But don't you see he could get *caught?* He bought the music downtown."

"So what?" Rachel shook her head. "I can't see Mr. Hawkins hiring detectives. Really."

"We'll see," I said darkly. "Anyway, there's something weird about it. I'm surprised you don't see that, Rache. It wasn't like Dooley." I didn't want to have to say outright that the energy, initiative, and imagination that the prank had taken were not characteristic of Dooley. That would have been tactless. But I hoped Rachel would get my point anyway.

"Well, I guess I've never known him to play a joke like that," she admitted.

"Aha, so you agree!" I leaned back on my elbows and frowned at her. "Do you have any idea what's behind this massive personality change?"

"Of course not," she snapped. "I can't read his mind."

"But doesn't he tell you what he's thinking about?" I insisted. "For a while there you two were eating lunch together all the time."

She avoided my eyes. "Not so much lately."

"Aha!" I jabbed a finger at her. "This could be significant."

Rachel slammed her French book closed. "Would you quit saying 'Aha!' You're driving me crazy. *What* could be significant?"

"That Dooley is acting *weird*. He is definitely not himself."

"Just because he's dumped me doesn't mean he's out of his mind, you know," she said bitterly. "He wouldn't be the first."

"Oh, stop it, Rache. He's crazy about you. He told me himself that he fell for you like a ton of bricks."

"He did?" She sat up. "When? What did he say? Tell me more! Much more. Don't leave anything out."

"I'm not real clear about the details, but he said he had fallen for somebody and the next thing I knew he was hanging around you, so I drew the logical conclusion."

"I used to think he liked me too," she said sadly. "But now—nothing. I don't even run into him at school anymore. It's like he's dropped down an open manhole. He's just—gone."

"But don't you see?" I insisted. "This is another example of a sudden change in his behavior. I think we need to find out what's going on with him."

Rachel looked doubtful.

"It could be something serious. Even"—I lowered my voice—"drugs."

"Yeah, but I don't know how we can draw somebody out if he doesn't want to talk to us."

"Piece of cake," I said. "Since you're grounded, I'll take care of it. I'll make some excuse to go over to his house, and I'll bet he'll open right up to me—if P.J. and Chris aren't around."

"I don't understand why you're so worried about Dooley all of a sudden." Her eyes narrowed.

"I have a purely humanitarian interest. That's all."

"That better be all."

"That's all that it is! Honest! What I feel for Dooley is strictly sisterly. He's not my type. Calm down. You ought to know that it's Pete I'm after." I twisted a strand of hair around my finger and considered it. "How do you think I'd look with a hair rinse? I could go from ordinary auburn to flamboyant flame."

"I thought we were talking about Dooley."

"Yeah, but if you're going to get weird about it, we can talk about something else."

"I'm not weird about it."

"Being grounded is making you paranoid, then."

Rachel slumped and the pile of magazines beside her bed leaned dangerously. I watched the stack nervously. Someday it was going to fall over and lives would be lost, possibly even mine.

"You're right, Andie," Rachel said. "I guess I am

19

getting paranoid. It's being grounded and then Dooley disappearing. I'm beginning to think I was born to be dumped." Rachel's guinea pig, alarmed by her tone of voice, squeaked and skittered under his hay.

"I don't think Dooley's really dumping you, Rache. He's crazy about you. He's just got something on his mind. Don't worry. I'll get on it right away and get it all fixed up."

"Sure, you will." Rachel fiddled with the fringe on her bedspread. "So, you and Pete are going out this weekend."

"Yeah." I sighed happily.

"I remember going out," she said plaintively. "It was fun."

"Cheer up, Rache. You won't be grounded forever."

"It already feels like forever."

I scrambled to my feet. "I'd better be going."

"Say hello to Pete for me," she said gloomily. "I guess you two are going to be a hot item now. I guess I'll be sitting by myself in the cafeteria from now on, all alone, picking at my food. I'll probably lose pounds and pounds"—her gaze settled on her bony legs— "which I can ill afford."

"He just asked me out for this one play," I said. "I don't know that this is going to develop into anything steady."

"It will," said Rachel.

"And even if it does, you and I can still eat lunch together."

It's amazing how easy it is to be optimistic about other people's romances, I thought as I walked home. I was sure Rachel would patch it up with Dooley. She was sure I would get something going with Pete.

Maybe I was unconsciously influenced by her point

of view or something because I went home feeling fairly cheerful. Or maybe it was because I had decided to help Dooley. It is very true that the best way to forget your own worries is to help somebody else. Poor orphaned Dooley. My heart bled for him. But with the support of his friends, he should be able to cope with his unsettling personality change. I was sure that when he told me all about what was on his mind, he'd feel much better. And if Pete and I became a hot item, I smiled, well, that would be just perfect.

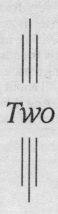

Two

It took me awhile to think of an excuse to drop by Dooley's house. In the end I only came up with a very weak one, but I told myself it didn't matter. It was only a device to get him alone anyway. Surely Dooley would be too involved in his personality change to bother picking holes in my story.

As it happened, Dooley sat behind me in algebra class. It was not something I normally thought about, because he sort of dozed all period. But now I realized that our accidental proximity would come in handy. My plan was to tell him I had picked up his algebra book by mistake. That was plausible. Of course, once I offered him the book he would check to see that he already had his book. But all I needed was a moment or two alone with him. "Anything bothering you, Dooley?" I would inquire in a perfectly natural way.

With any luck he would pour out his heart to me right on the spot just the way people do on soap operas.

I rehearsed my own lines in my mind as I trudged up the road to Dooley's house.

When I got there, I noticed a strange car parked next to Dooley's Jeep, a little blue Nissan. Did he already have a visitor? I hesitated. What the heck, I decided. I had come this far. I might as well see what was going on. I lifted the door knocker and slapped it against its brass base.

The door swung open at once, and I found myself facing a blond girl wearing earrings made out of curled bits of ribbon in the three primary colors. I could hardly take my eyes off the earrings, and it took me a moment to realize that not only was this a person I had never seen before, but Dooley's house looked all different. I couldn't see the usual heap of dirty dishes in the kitchen. And what had happened to Dooley's straw mat? A rug had replaced it on the living room floor. Where was the bicycle Dooley kept hung over the television? I felt as if I were losing my bearings.

"I'm sorry," I said awkwardly. "I'm looking for Dooley MacKenzie."

She smiled. "Oh, he's here." She turned. "Dooley!"

I realized that she was checking me out. I was curious about her, too, but I tried not to be so obvious about it. She was a little taller than me, slender, and wearing pale jeans.

Dooley shuffled out into the living room, barefoot, his hands in his pockets. He said something I didn't catch.

"A friend is here to see you," said the girl in an overly sweet voice.

Dooley blinked. "Andie! What are you doing here?"

I could feel hot blood rush to my face. Why didn't things ever go the way I planned? "I, uh, think I accidentally picked up your algebra book in class today."

He took the book from me and frowned. "Thanks."

"Don't you want to ask your friend in?" The blond girl was eyeing me from under her mascaraed lashes.

"Oh, I've got to be going," I said.

"'Bye," said Dooley with finality. He closed the door right in my face.

I stood there a moment, stunned. Not only had he been unbelievably rude, but he had taken my algebra book! He was supposed to look at it and then give it back to me—that was the plan. But he had grabbed it. Now, how was I going to do my homework?

I stomped home. What had got into Dooley? He was acting like a complete jerk. I mean, I know I had said he was undergoing a massive personality change, but this was ridiculous.

Suddenly a thought stopped me in my tracks. Rachel obviously didn't know about the blonde! How was I going to break it to her? That girl didn't look as if she had stopped by to borrow a cup of sugar either. She had answered the door. She was definitely at home there.

The one thing that was clear in my mind was that I didn't want to be the one to tell Rachel. I didn't see why I had to. Since she was grounded, it could be weeks before she found out. And after all, this whole thing with Dooley was quietly petering out. She told me herself that she never saw him anymore. After a few weeks she'd realize it was over, and then she'd calmly face the fact that he had found himself a new girl. At least, that was what I hoped.

When I got home, I found my mother in the kitchen eating her favorite snack, an apple. She had a theory that the smell of apples gave writers inspiration. According to her, Agatha Christie swore by them. It was a peculiar theory of literature, but it seemed to work for her. She was sniffing meditatively at the apple. She must have run into a tough spot with her story. "A boy called for you a minute ago," she said.

"Was it Chris?" Chris was always calling, either to get the name of some girl who was in my homeroom or else to tell me about the latest in his love life.

Mom glanced at the memo pad. "Nope. It was Pete Joyner. He said you had his number."

My knees locked. Maybe Pete was calling to cancel our date? "Should I call him, do you think?" I asked. "Or maybe I should wait for him to call back." I hesitated. "Yes, I'll wait for him to call back. I don't want to seem too eager."

Mom looked at me as if I had gone berserk. "Good grief, Andie!"

"Okay, I'll *call* him, Mom. Are you happy?"

I stomped upstairs. Then I realized I was acting just like P.J., an awful realization. So I forced myself to take a deep breath and calm down. The thing is I naturally couldn't help being somewhat churned up about this thing with Pete. At stake here was the whole question of whether I was going to spend my junior year as the gang's mascot or in the infinitely more rewarding role of femme fatale.

I got ahold of Pete right away.

"I just remembered," he said, "that I didn't tell you

when I'd pick you up." He laughed, a sound vaguely like distant thunder. A thrill of pleasure shot through me. The funny thing was that these days Pete's size gave me a weird kick. I was probably getting in touch with cavewoman-type feelings that dated back to the days girls sized up guys according to their ability to fight off saber-toothed tigers. Pete was one of the few guys I would have backed to win against the tiger.

We spoke of many things—what an idiot Mr. Hawkins was, how it was rumored someone was running a black market in used batteries, how we were going to flunk French if we weren't careful. I put my feet up on the bed and luxuriated in the sensation of being appreciated. Everything in my bedroom seemed softer and more lovely, as if life were being shot through a soft-focus lens. Either I was falling in love, or I was suffering from some very rare neurological disorder.

My door rattled. "Are you ever going to get off the phone?" P.J. yelled. "Other people have to use it, you know."

I hastily said goodbye to Pete. "I'm off!" I yelled as soon as I hung up.

"About time!" yelled P.J.

I sighed. This sordid scene only bore out my conclusion that it was infinitely better to be a girlfriend than a mere friend or stepsister. I wondered if there was any chance I could persuade Mom and Richard we desperately needed another phone line.

The phone rang, and I snatched it up. It was Rachel.

"Guess what?" she shrieked. "I'm ungrounded. Is that terrific, or what? I could tell Mom was weakening, you know? Like, she's been letting you come over to study and all, but suddenly just now she said she guessed I had learned my lesson and that they were going to commute my sentence to time served. How about that?"

It hit me that now that Rachel was able to go out, she was likely to find out about Dooley's blonde. Consequently, my joy at hearing her news was very short-lived. "That's great, Rache," I said in a faint voice. "Really."

"This is celebration time! Let's go to Appleby's and split a slice of apple pie, okay?"

"Are you two going to talk all night?" P.J. had picked up the downstairs extension. "I mean, other people have rights around here, you know. You've been on the phone an hour already, Andie."

"Twenty minutes," I protested. "Thirty at the most. Hang on, Rachel. I'm coming over. I'm on my way."

Yes, we definitely needed another phone line.

A few minutes later Rachel and I piled into her mom's Volvo and headed toward Appleby's. Surreptitiously, I shot Rachel a sympathetic look. At least, I thought, this time it won't be a sudden shock the way it was when Chris dumped her. She already suspects Dooley's affection is waning. And just because she isn't grounded anymore doesn't mean she's going to start trailing Dooley around and spying on him. It could be days and days before she found out about his other girl.

Rachel turned a corner sharply. "Guess what?" she burbled. "You'll never guess! I've heard from Dooley. We're going out to dinner tomorrow night. He apologized for not calling before and said he had a lot on his mind, so I guess you were right, Andie. Something *is* bothering him."

My mouth fell open. Dooley was going out with

Rachel while keeping the blonde on the side? This was a twist I hadn't foreseen. Of course, maybe he was planning to break up with Rachel formally. Should I prepare her for the shock?

The Volvo tooled on down the bluff. Chris passed us in his mom's white Toyota and honked. I couldn't see who was with him. It was hard to keep up with Chris's girls when they had a shelf life of mere days.

Rachel sniffed. "I'm certainly glad Dooley isn't like Chris. I know I was completely taken in by Chris. You don't have to remind me. But good looks just don't do it for me anymore. Kindness, understanding, sensitivity—those are the really important things, right?"

"Absolutely," I said feebly.

"I mean, if you can't trust a guy, what have you got?"

Thinking of the blonde at Dooley's house, I was at a loss for words. Luckily, Rachel took my silence for agreement.

When we got to Appleby's, we took a booth and ordered apple pie and two plates.

When our order came, Rachel tucked her dark hair behind her ears and began digging in. I felt a pang of pity as I watched her innocently enjoying her apple pie.

"The thing with Dooley, Andie, is that we're so close. Of course, since I've been grounded we haven't been able to actually go out, but we've had a few lovely moments together back by the engineering building. And those lunches together under the stairs on A wing." She sighed. "The thing with Dooley and me is that we actually talk to each other. That's why it seemed so strange when he just disappeared. I didn't know what to think. We were close, you know? And then nothing. But I'm sure he's had a good reason. Tomorrow night he'll tell me all about it. I mean, I hate to think what he must have been going through if he was too upset to talk to me. But I know that whatever it was, he didn't mean to hurt me. Perfect trust, that's where it's at. Hey, you aren't eating!"

I prodded the pie into crumbs with my fork. "Rachel, don't you think that if a person is happy, then that's the main thing?"

"I guess. What are you getting at?"

"I mean, knowing the whole truth is not necessarily conducive to happiness. Like my mother is sort of lost in a fantasy world all the time writing those dumb books of hers, but she's happy."

"I don't follow you. What does your mother have to do with my love life?"

I saw that I would have to be more direct. "Like," I began hesitantly, "say for example that somebody I like is cheating on me—well, maybe I'm better off not knowing, right?"

She licked her spoon and grinned. "But how can you rip out his heart and boil it in oil if you don't even know about it?"

I chuckled nervously. Once my mother had taken me to a college production of *Othello* and the grisly flavor of it was coming back to me. "Yeah, but the thing is if you don't know you wouldn't even want to rip out his heart, right? I mean, think about Othello. Like, at one point he says even if his wife were fooling around with every soldier in camp, he'd be happy if he didn't know about it."

"Isn't he the dude who killed his wife when he thought she was cheating on him? I don't get it, Andie.

What's all this morbid interest in people cheating on people? Is something wrong between you and Pete?"

"Fine, everything's fine. We talked for a long time today, and we're still going to that play this weekend."

"Well, then." She looked around for the waitress. "What do you say we split an order of fries."

When the waitress left, Rachel leaned her chin on her hand and smiled beatifically. "To think that yesterday everything was awful—I was grounded, I thought Dooley had dumped me. Now suddenly everything is totally perfect."

"Dooley's got another girl," I blurted out.

"What!"

I hadn't really intended to come out with it that way. "I don't know what made me say that," I gulped.

Rachel didn't even seem to notice when the waitress laid the plate of fries down in front of her. "Perhaps you said it because it was the truth?" she said icily. "Tell me everything. And I mean every single grim detail."

I didn't like her tone. I was getting these Othello vibes all over again. "Well," I said, "I went over there today to draw Dooley out, the way I said I was going to do—by the way, I need to borrow your algebra book."

Rachel tapped her fork on her plate impatiently. "Get to the point, Andie."

"So this girl answered the door."

"Who was it? I'll bet it was Sally Howe, wasn't it? I've seen her looking at him." Rachel's eyes narrowed.

"I don't know who it was. I've never seen her before in my life."

"Of course, you don't know all that many people yet." She frowned. "Do you think it could be Millicent Crawford? She's a blonde."

I shrugged helplessly.

Rachel gritted her teeth. "When I think of how I felt sorry for him, how I *worried* about him, how I missed him. How could I have been such an idiot!"

"You don't think this girl could have been a maid, do you?" I asked doubtfully.

"Was she wearing an apron and driving an old car?"

"No."

"Then she couldn't have been a maid," said Rachel. "What made you even think of such a dumb thing?"

"Well, I've always said Dooley needed help on the housework, and I think this girl had been washing the dishes. I mean, they were all clean, and you know how Dooley only washes dishes on Friday."

"She'd been washing dishes!" screeched Rachel.

I looked around nervously. "Cut it out, Rache. People are staring."

Rachel tore her napkin into tiny pieces. "She's moved in!" she wailed. Unfortunately, Rachel was not one to hold her emotions in check. "I can't believe it! It can't be Sally Howe. Her parents would kill her if she moved in with Dooley. It must be somebody older. Did she look like maybe she was in junior college or something?"

"I don't know. I was so busy taking it all in—these weird earrings she was wearing, all the dishes clean and all. I just couldn't say, Rache."

"My mom always said something like this was going to happen with Dooley on his own all the time. How could I have been such an idiot? How could I have trusted him?"

I eyed her uneasily. "You're going to break the date, I guess."

"Certainly not. I have to plot my revenge." She

picked up a french fry, considered it, then savagely bit it in two.

"Don't do anything you're going to regret," I said uneasily. "There are laws, you know."

"I don't know what I'm going to do yet." She frowned. "But something good."

I figured it was time we left Appleby's. The waitress had the look of someone who was about to dial 911. Not for the first time, I wished that Rachel were the sort of person who rolled with the punches.

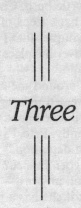

Three

Pete caught up with me after my second-period class. He grabbed my hand and pulled me down the hall. "I called you back, but P.J. said you had gone out and weren't ever coming back."

"He's kind of funny about me using the phone. I guess he's not used to sharing it yet. What were you calling about?"

"Just to talk." He grinned. "I really liked talking to you."

"Me too. Uh, where are we going?"

"We're taking a detour by the engineering building. Lucky there are still a few private places in this school where a guy and a girl can talk."

The engineering building, the outbuilding where drafting and mechanical drawing were taught, wasn't nearly so private as Pete seemed to think. The bushes were stirring with other couples who were likewise seeking privacy. I saw P.J. making out with Susie Skinner behind a myrtle bush. Chris was sitting with Ann Shafley on the back steps of the building. And those were only the couples that I recognized. People were making out all over the place until I didn't know which way to look.

Pete put his arms around me and drew me close, until my nose was pressed tight against the button of his shirt. "Mmm, you smell good," he said.

"I shampoo frequently. Pete, I've got to get to class. I can't afford to get a detention."

"What have you got? French? Cut it. She never remembers to take roll anyway."

"I know, but what if she has a pop test?"

Pete lifted me high in the air. "So you miss it."

I giggled nervously. "Put me down."

"Don't worry, I'm not going to drop you."

I felt as if I had been grabbed by some friendly but unruly bear. I could see over the top of the myrtle bush. P.J. and Susie Skinner were certainly exceedingly friendly. I averted my eyes, my knees rigid with fear. I have never cared for heights, and I began finding it hard to breathe.

"Please, Pete," I pleaded.

He put me down gently.

"I've really got to go," I said.

"I didn't scare you, did I?" He looked unhappy. "It's just so great to finally meet up with somebody that I have a lot in common with, you know?"

I took his hands and squeezed them. "Oh, I know. I feel the same way. Really. The only thing is"—I glanced down at my watch—"I've only got two and a half minutes to get to French class."

"Okay. You'd better go."

I hesitated. The last thing I wanted to do was come across as rejecting him. "So I guess I'll go now, okay?"

He smiled at me. "It's okay. Go."

I turned and took off running. But I didn't make it to class in time. The bell rang just as I was rounding the corner of A wing. I stood in front of Madame Vanderwort's locked door and swore softly. It was just possible that being a femme fatale was going to prove somewhat more tricky than I had anticipated.

I turned and trudged to the office. Judging by the number of people lined up for admit slips, the school was full of people who thought detention was a small price to pay for a few stolen moments of bliss behind the engineering building.

Leaving the office, I passed P.J. He grinned at me. "Pete and Andie sitting in a tree, k-i-s-s-i-n-g . . ."

"P.J.," I said, "that remark is beneath you. About ten years beneath you."

"Ow." He slapped his hand to his chest and twisted slowly to the floor. "Did you hear that, Susie? She thinks I'm immature. It hurts, oh, it hurts. Oh, oh, I'm done for."

Susie Skinner just stood there giggling while I hurried off to Madame Vanderwort's class.

Chris rode home with P.J. and me that afternoon. Although he borrowed his mom's car sometimes, more often he rode home from school with us. I was extremely relieved that he didn't mention seeing me behind the engineering building too. I found the whole thing somewhat embarrassing. I glanced behind us, expecting to see Dooley's Jeep. "Where's Dooley?" I asked.

"Don't ask," said P.J.

I looked at them both uneasily. "Does this have something to do with a girl, by any chance?"

Chris and P.J. shrugged in unison.

"A female anyway," said Chris.

"Cut it out, guys. Tell me. What's the big secret?"

"No secret," said P.J. "Dooley's got to go get a haircut."

I thought about that. "Okay, he could use a haircut. Where does the female come in?"

"It's Dooley's dad's girlfriend," said Chris cryptically.

"Dooley's dad's girlfriend is taking him to get a haircut? Why would she do that?"

"Don't ask me," said P.J. "She's doing all kinds of things. I went by there the other day and she'd put up curtains." He shook his head. "Give a woman an inch and she'll take a mile."

Suddenly I felt a sinking feeling. "Wait a minute— is Dooley's dad's girlfriend a blonde?"

"Dunno," said P.J. "Haven't met the lady."

"I have," said Chris. "She's kind of cute. Only thing is, she's got some kind of crazy idea that Dooley needs a mother. Ever since she moved in, she's changing everything around. She keeps blathering about feeding him fresh vegetables too. I think she's a vegetarian or something."

"The trouble started when Dooley's dad got that promotion," said P.J.

"You're right," said Chris. "Kind of makes you stop and think, doesn't it? I mean, is success worth all this? Dooley never had a bit of trouble until his dad got branch manager a couple weeks ago and quit having to travel so much. Now his dad's around the house all the time and this woman is too. They're driving Dooley out of his mind."

"You might have mentioned it before now." I was rearranging my thoughts hastily. The blonde belonged not to Dooley but his dad?

"None of our business, of course. Strictly Dooley's problem." P.J. glared at me sternly. "It's none of your business either, Andie."

"Rachel!" I cried.

"Nope, Rachel is Dooley's girlfriend," P.J. corrected me. "His dad's girlfriend is named Terri, I think."

"P.J." I grabbed his arm. "I saw that woman over at Dooley's house, and I told Rachel, and now she's trying to figure out some way to get back at Dooley for having another girl!" I groaned.

"That's the sort of thing that happens when you mess with other people's business," said Chris.

I glared at him. Why did life have to be so complicated? Rachel wasn't grounded, I was well on my way to having a boyfriend, and suddenly everything was more of a mess than it had ever been.

As soon as we got home, I dashed over to Rachel's house, but she wasn't there.

"I'll tell her you came by," said Rachel's mom.

"No. Just tell her that everything I told her about Dooley was all wrong."

"Everything you told her about Dooley was all wrong," repeated Mrs. Green. She glanced at her watch.

"Right. You won't forget, will you?"

Mrs. Green smiled at me. "I'm on my way out. I'll leave her a note."

Not good enough, I thought. What if she misses seeing it?

"Do you happen to know what time she's going out with Dooley?" I asked.

"I'm afraid not," she said.

Mrs. Green was so calm she made me want to scream. But there was nothing I could do but go home.

I stood at the window of my bedroom for what seemed like ages watching for Rachel's car. Only one main road went up the bluff, and it passed directly in front of our house. So if Rachel had gone anywhere outside of the immediate neighborhood, she would have to drive right by the house where I could see her.

Then I had a horrible thought. What if she hadn't gone out of the neighborhood at all? What if she had gone to booby-trap Dooley's Jeep—or even his house?

By the time I finally saw the Volvo drive up the road and turn in at Rachel's house, I had been pacing back and forth so long I had practically worn a hole in the carpet. I ran downstairs. Outside shadows were closing in on the beige lawns and the shrubbery of the neighborhood. I could only make out the pale oval of Rachel's face as she lifted some packages out of the car. I ran over to her.

"Andie!" she exclaimed as I skidded to a stop at her side. "What's wrong?"

"Everything I told you about Dooley is all wrong," I panted. "There is no other girl."

"There isn't?" She looked at me blankly. "Then who is the blonde?"

"Dooley's father's girlfriend."

"But I thought that all Dooley's father's girlfriends lived other places—like Tarboro and Charlotte."

"Not anymore. Dooley's dad isn't traveling these

days. I just found out about it myself. He's been promoted to branch manager, and now he's in town all the time and his girlfriend has moved in with him."

"Of course," she said grudgingly. "I'm glad to hear that."

"I thought you would be."

"But how did you get it mixed up in the first place?"

"It was because nobody ever tells me anything," I said. "If Chris or P.J. had just told me that Dooley's dad's girlfriend was living over there, I wouldn't have gotten mixed up. You'd think it was a state secret or something."

"I guess Dooley's sort of embarrassed about it, don't you think? I mean, you don't think of somebody's father having a girlfriend."

"Oh, I don't know about that. Mom was Richard's girlfriend until they got married. Not that she moved in with him or anything."

"That's different. Your mother's a *mother,* not some ditsy blonde. Look, I'm freezing. What are we doing standing outside like this?"

We went inside and Rachel dropped her packages on the floor of the foyer. As she struggled out of her jacket, I spotted a bucket of water sitting in the corner of the foyer.

"What's that?" I asked.

"What?" Rachel turned around. "Oh, that's just the bucket of cold water I was going to throw in Dooley's face, that's all. Lucky thing you got to me in time."

I shuddered. "Rachel, have you ever thought about trying to be more laid back?"

"No," she said shortly. "Have you ever thought about being more accurate?"

"I'm sorry, but it was a perfectly understandable mistake."

"I accept your apology, such as it is."

I followed Rachel up to her room. "I guess you must be pretty relieved to find out that Dooley hasn't been cheating on you after all, huh?"

"Actually, I'm having trouble sort of adjusting my thoughts, you know? I have to keep reminding myself that Dooley is not a two-timing creep."

"I'm really sorry, Rache."

"People can't be jerked around all the time and come out feeling just the same. Do you follow me?"

"I do," I said penitently. "I'm deeply sorry. I do most humbly abase myself. Truly. It won't happen again."

"Like, suppose you did something like that to Pete—" she began.

"Pete!" I went rigid.

"Pete Joyner," she repeated patiently. "Remember him?"

"Yikes, I forgot," I shrieked. "I'm supposed to be going to dinner with him right now!"

I tore down the marble staircase and ran home. I found Pete was sitting in our living room making awkward conversation with my mom.

"Andie!" cried Mom. "Where have you been? Pete's been waiting for you, and I didn't even know where you'd gone to."

"I just ran next door a minute. Hang on, Pete, I have to go change my clothes."

"Sure," he said. He looked at me with sad brown basset hound eyes.

I ran upstairs and changed into the most smashing

thing I owned. When I came downstairs, Pete seemed slightly more cheerful.

"I'm really sorry I'm late," I said. "I had to run next door to Rachel's. It was important."

"Sure, no big deal."

"I don't want you to think I forgot or anything. It's just that something came up."

He took my hands in his enormous paws. "I understand, Andie. Don't worry about it." His brown eyes looked into mine, and I could feel myself melting. I made a silent vow that in the future I would *always* be on time when he came.

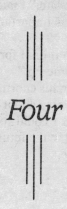

Four

On our way to the restaurant I told Pete all about what had happened with Dooley.

"The poor guy," he said sympathetically. "I really feel sorry for kids from broken homes. If your parents are tearing around all over the place with a messy love life of their own, how do they expect you to get it all together? I don't think parents ought to behave like that."

I had to agree that it would be perfect if parents didn't have messy love lives. Ideally, parents should do their romancing before kids are born and be done with it. But unfortunately, it didn't always work out that neatly. For instance, in my case, my father, the race car driver, managed to get blown up in a fiery crash when I was only six. I figured it wasn't reasonable to expect my mom to spend the rest of her life doing nothing but read *Peter Rabbit* and go to PTA meetings.

"I guess all this explains why MacKenzie's gone to pieces lately," Pete said.

I was startled. "Dooley's gone to pieces?"

"He doesn't even comb his hair, Andie. And those jeans of his—I know tears are supposed to be cool, but when it comes to seeing people's underwear, I think it's too much."

"I hadn't noticed," I said guiltily. Of course, Pete's jeans had actual creases in them. It was very possible he was exaggerating the defects in Dooley's grooming.

We went to Hunan's Chinese Garden. There we ate moo goo gai pan and talked about the rotten teachers we had had, a pretty much bottomless subject. It turned out we both had had to read *The Call of the Wild* in the ninth grade and we both had hated it.

"My brother was crazy about it," said Pete, "so I got my hopes up. What a disappointment!"

"I didn't know you had an older brother. Is he away at college?"

"Nope. He's a wilderness guide up in Alaska. I don't understand why people want to do crazy things like dropping out of college to go off to Alaska. All this survival of the fittest stuff leaves me cold." He grinned. "Literally."

"Me too. I personally like warm baths too much to be a wilderness guide in Alaska."

"I'm with you. The problem is there aren't enough people in the world who have simple, basic, common sense."

I looked at him in amazement. I had thought that exact thing so many times! It was uncanny. "I couldn't agree with you more."

"Like in *Romeo and Juliet*. Have you ever seen that?"

I nodded. Maybe it was because my mom was a writer, but any time there was anything remotely literary going on I got taken to it, whether I wanted to or not.

"I saw the movie," said Pete. "On cassette. Another one of my brother's recommendations." He sighed. "I wonder when I'm going to catch on that if he likes it, that means I won't. The thing is we aren't alike at all. Not a bit. My brother thought it was so hot and sexy, and I'm sitting there the whole time thinking—these idiots!"

"Oh, me too," I said eagerly. "It looks like instead of killing themselves they could have moved to another town, and Romeo could have gotten a good job in the post office. I just hated the ending."

He grabbed my hands. "Andie, do you believe in love at first sight?"

"I guess." I eyed him with faint uneasiness. Were we still talking about *Romeo and Juliet*?

He took a deep breath. "I mean, I think people ought to get to know each other and all. That only makes sense."

"Absolutely. Like with Romeo and Juliet. Their meeting on a balcony and throwing around a little blank verse. Well, how well can you really get to know each other that way?"

"Yeah, but still, don't you think you can just be drawn to somebody, that you can feel right from the start that this is the one?"

"I guess it's possible," I said cautiously. The fact that Pete was holding my hands naturally led me to wonder if what he was saying had a personal application.

"I think when people are right for each other, they have a kind of instinct that lets them recognize each other," he said.

I had the uneasy sensation that Pete might not be as different from his brother as he thought he was. I spotted distinct signs of rampant romanticism. And I should be able to recognize the symptoms. My own mother was an advanced case. Why else had she married a race car driver?

"I think you were right the first time," I said. "It's better to get to know each other a little at a time. I mean, that was the mistake Romeo and Juliet made, right? Jumping into love with both feet."

"You're right," said Pete. "But the thing is you can fall in love and then get to know each other afterward. There's nothing crazy about that."

When the waitress brought the check and two fortune cookies, Pete moved closer to the ten-watt lamp on the wall and began going over the waitress's addition. I was glad to see that the romantic side of him had retreated and the practical side had come forward once more. I felt much more able to deal with that.

As soon as he had finished calculating the tip, he broke his fortune cookie open.

"What does it say?" I asked.

A slow smile spread across his face. He put the fortune on the table in front of me and smoothed it out with his fingers.

I strained to read it in the dim light. "You are about to begin an exciting romance," it said.

I gulped.

"So, what about yours?" he asked.

I cracked my fortune cookie, but I was so jittery I let the slip of paper fall to the floor. "Oh, dear, I dropped it." I peered below the table but couldn't find it. The restaurant had the illumination of your average bat cave.

Pete glanced at his watch. "Well, don't look for it, Andie. We'd better go. We don't want to be late for the play."

Maybe it was just as well about my losing the fortune. If mine had matched Pete's, he might have leapt right over the table at me. I had never thought of fortune cookies as a high-risk enterprise before that night, but then I was just learning the ropes of this boyfriend-girlfriend stuff.

It turned out *The Actor and the Assassin* was about John Wilkes Booth. It was pretty good, actually. But I found it hard to concentrate. I kept thinking about what Pete had said. When he said he believed in love at first sight, was he speaking generally or extremely particularly? This is the kind of thought that makes it extremely difficult to concentrate on any play, however good.

Pete helped me into my coat afterward. We forged through the crowd and plunged outside into the darkness. "Brrr," he said. "This is when I start thinking I'd like to move to southern California." He put his arm around me and drew me close. "What do you think, Andie? You think you'd like to live in California?"

"What about those earthquakes?"

"We'll have to check those out before we do anything." He laughed and gave me a squeeze. A moment

46

later I surreptitiously patted my sides and ascertained that there were no broken ribs.

"So, what'd you think of the play?" he asked.

"Nice. Very good," I said. I was still working on "You think you'd like California?" Were we merely discussing the weather? I wasn't sure, but ever since the fortune cookie incident I was on the alert for personal comments.

"It looks like snow," Pete observed as we drove out of the parking lot.

"Mmm." I snuggled down in my coat. The streetlights had frosty little halos of fog.

At the stoplight Pete leaned over and kissed my cold nose. Suddenly everything became crystal clear to me. It was like a burst of revelation. The important thing was to live for the moment! That was the answer. I felt the truth of this even more strongly at the next light when he took my hand and smiled at me. I got warm all over, a feeling not entirely due to the fact that the car heater was finally kicking in.

After we reached my house, we paused on the doorstep and kissed. A few snowflakes drifted down in the porch light, and I snuggled close to Pete. His body gave off warmth like a banked fire.

"Did you have fun?" he murmured in my ear.

"I had a lovely time." A flake fell on my nose and I sneezed.

"Me too." He gave me a quick hug. "You'd better get on inside. We don't want you to catch cold."

The more I thought about it, the more it seemed that falling in love was a very good idea. It just needed a little getting used to. Hugging, kissing—those were wonderful things. Why worry? Still glowing, I went in and made for the kitchen. I had the idea I would get a glass of milk before collapsing into bed. Mom and Richard were sitting in the kitchen. They had been to some business function or another. Mom kicked her dress shoes off. She was sitting by the phone yawning. Richard was casing the contents of the refrigerator. I could have told him the odds of finding anything choice were not good. "Did you kids have fun?" he asked.

I nodded.

"I like your Pete," Mom said. "He's a very sensible boy. He knows what he wants and he's willing to work for it. He told me he plans to be an accountant. I believe there are a lot of good opportunities in that field."

"Is this the only thing we've got to eat?" asked Richard. "Curried chickpeas? I don't call that food."

"It's absolutely wonderful for your cholesterol," Mom said.

Richard made a rude noise.

"There ought to be cold cuts and things in there," Mom said.

"There are *not* any cold cuts. There is one half piece of bologna." Richard examined it closely. "And I think it's moldy."

The cupboard was bare again. P.J. and his friends had gotten there first. It was nice not to be the only victim.

"I'll go shopping tomorrow," Mom promised.

"I can't wait until tomorrow. I'm hungry now." Richard put the chickpeas in the microwave. "Andie, I hear terrific things about Pete from his dad. He says Pete's very responsible, a very solid kid, not like that older boy of theirs who's paddling a canoe somewhere

48

up in Alaska. It's nice to know you're out with a boy we don't have to worry about."

Mom dimpled. "Richard had a wild youth. That's why he always thinks the worst of boys."

"That's not it," Richard protested. "It's just that you've got to admit there are some pretty wild kids around." Richard looked at the clock and frowned. "Which reminds me—I wonder where P.J. is. Doesn't that girl of his have a curfew? What kind of parents does she have?"

"Anyway," my mom put in, "we like Pete very much."

I discovered that this shower of parental approval rather put a damper on my romantic mood. I tried, however, to take it in the spirit it was offered. "He's very well organized," I said. "He gave me an appointment calendar to help me get my life under control. He says I tend to overschedule."

"Chris called while you were out," Mom said.

I put the milk carton back in the fridge. "I'd better go up and call him back."

"He certainly seems to call you a lot," said Mom.

"He's my phone-friend, Mom. I give him the female point of view, something he really needs."

"I thought he was P.J.'s friend," she said.

"P.J. is busy these days," I said. "In case you haven't noticed." The microwave went *ping*.

Richard frowned, but I wasn't sure whether it was about P.J.'s intense involvement with Susie Skinner or the prospect of eating all those curried chickpeas.

I took my glass of milk upstairs and called Chris.

"Where were you?" he asked querulously. "I called you hours ago."

"I was out with Pete Joyner," I said. "Mom and Richard just *adore* him. They're ready to ask him to move in with us."

"Rah-rah-rah!"

"What's the matter with you?"

"Did I say anything was the matter?"

"You sound like you're in a pretty bad mood," I said.

"Liz dumped me!"

"Liz who?"

"Liz Raymond, idiot. Don't you listen to anything I tell you?"

I did vaguely remember something about Chris going to hang out around the stables in the hope of picking up this girl who was into horseback riding. But I thought her name was Lib. "Is she the one who likes horses?" I ventured.

"Yeah, and I tell you, the way she can control a ton of horseflesh, well, it's incredible, that's all."

"But you say she dumped you?"

"Can you believe it? She said I was too frivolous for her. Frivolous! Me!"

"Maybe it was for the best, Chris. Maybe she was not your type."

"Actually, I had been kind of thinking that. I mean, I'm as interested in horses as the next guy, but when that's all a girl talks about, it gets kind of boring, you know? I was thinking I would sort of cool things with her, but I never got the chance. She dumped me first. Do you think I'm frivolous, Andie?"

"How do you define frivolous?"

"Just give me a straight answer. Do I come across as the world's greatest fluff brain?"

"No."

"That's something, I guess," he said grudgingly. "Did you have a good time with what'shisname?"

"Pete. His name is Pete Joyner. Yes, I had a wonderful time. We ate Chinese and then saw a gripping drama at the playhouse."

"I just hope the guy didn't step on your toes. We'd have to scrape your little tootsies up off the floor."

I curled my feet under my body protectively. "Don't be ridiculous. Pete is extremely careful and very considerate. He would never step on my toes."

"I saw him throw you in the air back at the engineering building the other day."

"I'm amazed you noticed. I thought you were otherwise occupied."

"I was just having a serious discussion with Ann Shafley," he said with dignity. "Bet you *she* doesn't think I'm frivolous. You know what I'm thinking? Since Liz dumped me, I mean, I've been thinking about Fiona Burney. I went out with her at the beginning of last year, and I really liked her a lot."

"Why'd you break up with her, then?"

"Oh, I don't know. I guess it was just one of those things. No, wait—I remember now. It was because of Kelly Hemming. I saw Kelly standing on her head at the gymnastics trials, her face all pink, you know, and I was just gone. It was, like wow! An unbelievable experience. I kind of forgot about Fiona for a while, everything happened so fast with Kelly. You think Fiona might still be holding a grudge?"

"There's only one way to find out."

"You're right. I think I'll give her a call. You know, it's really a help to me to talk to you like this, Andie. I

51

don't mind telling you that after Liz dumped me I was pretty shook. Something like that really makes a guy stop and think, you know? Till now I've sort of figured, heck, I'm young. Why get tied down?"

"I know, I know. I'm going to embroider a pillow for you with that motto."

"Cut it out! You know what I mean."

"I'm afraid I don't see exactly what you're getting at." I yawned. "Also, I've got to get to bed. I'm very tired. I've had a big evening."

"It's just that I got this sort of cold chill after it happened, you know?"

"What kind of cold chill? I'm too tired to play guessing games, Chris."

His voice dropped half a register. "It's like this. It hit me, like, maybe it's time to grow up."

I grinned. "You'll feel better tomorrow."

"You think?"

"I'm sure of it."

I replaced the receiver firmly on its cradle.

Pete got in the habit of carrying my books to history class Monday and Tuesday. Also, we ate lunch together every day. Overnight we had become a couple. It was hard to believe that short days before I had been wondering if I would ever be able to attract a boy. Now I was smack in the middle of a full-scale romance. It felt good.

However, the next day when I carried my tray out of the lunch line, I spotted Rachel's forlorn face, and suddenly I was overcome with guilt. She had a paperback propped open with her milk carton. "I think I'd better eat lunch with Rachel today," I told Pete. "I've hardly seen her all week."

"Why doesn't Rachel just come over and eat lunch with us?"

"It's not the same thing. I think I need to cheer her up, and she doesn't know you that well. She may need to talk to me in private."

"What about cheering me up," he grumbled. But he took his tray over to a table of his friends without any further complaints.

Rachel glanced at me when I sat down across from her. "Hullo," she said. "I thought you had emigrated to Australia."

"It hasn't been *that* long since I've been around. Where's Dooley?"

"Cutting school. Honestly, Andie, it's awful. He's so upset. I can hardly believe how unhappy he is."

"He can't get used to having a normal home life, huh?"

"Just think about it," she said. "Here he's used to being on his own, and now all of a sudden everything is different. And it's so regimented. Scrambled eggs at seven, bean casserole at seven. This girlfriend of his father's has just taken over. She keeps asking him what he's going to do with his life. And if she's not harping on that, she's telling him he needs to work harder to bring up his grades."

"She may be right. His grades aren't the best."

"But it's none of her business!" Rachel cried. "How would you like it if some perfect stranger moved in and started telling you what to do?"

"Maybe he should try harder to adjust?" I suggested.

"Whose side are you on?" Rachel snapped.

"Yours," I said quickly. "Yours and Dooley's. But

he's sort of in a fix, isn't he? I mean, whatever's going on, he's pretty much got to make the best of it. It's not like he can get rid of her."

"Wrong!" said Rachel. "That's just what he's going to do. Get rid of her."

"How?" I stopped myself. "No, don't tell me how."

"Oh, don't worry. It's nothing illegal. Dooley doesn't think he has to do anything drastic. His father's just gone temporarily gaga. It's sort of a midlife crisis. Pretty soon this girlfriend will be history like all the rest of them." Rachel touched her fingertips together and smiled. "Of course, Dooley does have a few ideas on how to help the process along."

I wasn't sure I wanted to hear about Dooley's plans for getting rid of his father's girlfriend. The whole idea had begun to make me uncomfortable. Things at my own house were in a delicate balance, and I didn't want to rock the boat. It could be dangerous for me to start looking at things from Dooley's point of view. What if his discontent was catching? "That's all right," I said hastily. "Spare me the details."

Pete called me that afternoon after school—at four-thirty. He always called at four-thirty. He was very well organized. Also very punctual.

"Justin Henry asked me if we broke up," he said.

"Why would he ask you something like that?"

"Because we weren't eating lunch together. That's why."

"I don't see why we have to eat lunch together every day just to please Justin Henry."

"Don't you want to eat lunch with me, Andie?"

"Of course I do. You know I do."

"Okay, then. If you want to cheer Rachel up, just have her come eat with us the way I said."

There was a flaw in Pete's reasoning somewhere, but I couldn't seem to put my finger on it. "I just don't want to lose touch with my friends," I said.

"You don't have to lose touch with your friends. Didn't I say you could have Rachel come and eat with us?"

"Okay. I guess you're right."

After we hung up I went down to the kitchen and got a handful of pretzels, the last in the tin. I could hear someone down in the garage. When I opened the kitchen door and looked down the steps, I saw Chris working out on the NordicTrack. His eyes lit up when he spotted me. The sight of food often had that effect on him.

"You can't have any of my pretzels," I said, automatically putting them behind me. "These are the last ones. Besides, you aren't supposed to eat when you're working out." I went on downstairs.

"What do you know about it?" he retorted.

As soon as I sat down, Chris grabbed a pretzel out of my hand. "Let me tell you, working out isn't much fun when you have to do it by yourself," he said, biting into the pretzel.

"I know," I said sympathetically. "It's tough."

He glanced at me. "Have you ever thought about trying to get in better shape?" he pinched the flesh on my forearm. "You got a lot of flab there."

I drew away from him and carefully rearranged my

sweater. "That is not flab, that is relaxed muscle. More or less."

Chris snorted. "Less." His blond hair clung damply to his face and his face was flushed. Now that I was seeing so much of Pete, I noticed that Chris didn't look so tall as he had before. How true it is that everything is relative. Relative to Pete, everyone was *très petit,* as we said in French class.

"Chris," I said, "do you believe in love at first sight?"

He shrugged. "Sure. You know, like you see some babe across the room and bam, you're gone. You know me, Andie. I go for girls like that all the time."

"Yes, but *that* is not a mature affection. That's not the kind of thing I'm talking about. I'm talking more about the kind of thing Pete and I have."

Chris hooted. "So this thing you've got with Pete is super mature, huh?"

"Well, yes. It is."

"Give me a break! Take it from me, this time you're losing it."

"You think?" Suddenly I was uncertain.

"I'm serious. You left any kind of reality ten miles back."

"Wait a minute! What's *wrong* with what I was saying?"

"Okay, you and Pete eat lunch together every day. So what?"

"That's not all we do together."

"Look, I don't want to hear about it," he said sharply.

"I mean we go out together and stuff." I sensed that

Chris had been shaken by Liz dumping him. He was getting awfully touchy.

"Listen," he said, "what you two have going is a social arrangement. That's all there is to it. It's not 'mature.' It's not 'special.' It's just what everybody else happens to be doing. You've been brainwashed."

"Do you have to be so cynical? Don't you believe that zingy feeling a person gets when another person is around can be turned into a mature and long-lasting relationship?"

He grinned. "Not if I have anything to say about it."

"You're hopeless." I gave him a little shove. "What's happened to P.J. and Dooley?"

He made a face. "P.J.'s off with Susie Skinner, and God knows where Dooley is. Either with Rachel or off plotting against his dad's girlfriend, I guess. Maybe both. Dooley's got this idea that everything is the girlfriend's fault. She *makes* his father do this, she *makes* his father say that. As if his father didn't have a mind of his own."

"Maybe he doesn't."

Chris shrugged. "Everybody's got a mind of his own."

"But Dooley could be right. Maybe the woman is brainwashing his dad."

"So what if she is? There's nothing Dooley can do about it, and as far as I'm concerned, it all amounts to the same thing—Dooley's never around anymore. And I don't have to tell you the way things are with P.J."

I frowned. "It's terrible the way he's always off with Susie Skinner! I think it's such a mistake for people to get so wrapped up in their girlfriend that they lose touch with their friends."

He looked at me in surprise. "Hey, that's my line!"

"Okay, so I'm agreeing with you. Is that all right?"

He grinned. "Ol' Pete crowding you some, huh?"

"I didn't say that."

"You didn't have to. I've been there. First you're talking about love at first sight, next you're talking about a long-lasting relationship, and next you're checking the room for exits. Right?"

"I am not checking for exits," I said. "I am only giving some serious thought to this whole love issue. It's just like you to jump to conclusions."

"Look, just don't go telling me about love, okay? I could write a book. You're talking to an authority here."

I climbed up on the stationary bicycle, gave a desultory push to its pedal, looked down, and watched its shiny flywheel go round. "Yeah, but the thing is, love is sort of new to me. I've never really gone steady with anybody before."

"Stinks, doesn't it?" he said cheerfully.

"No!" I protested. "It's got its good points and its bad points, like anything else, but all in all I think it's nice. Being close to somebody makes you feel good. It's great to feel a part of things, not to be left out, you know. And I really like Pete. I really, really do."

"That's good. I'm really, really happy for you." He grinned.

"You are disgusting." I clambered down from the bicycle.

"Hey, where are you going?" he protested.

"To get a second opinion," I said over my shoulder.

* * *

I went over to Rachel's house. Not only was Chris opposed to romantic commitment of any sort, but he was not exactly impartial when it came to talking about Pete. And lately I did want to talk about Pete—constantly.

"It must be ESP!" Rachel exclaimed when I walked into her room. "I was just going to call you. Did you know that Mr. Hawkins had Dooley in his office this afternoon?"

I sat down suddenly on Rachel's bed, all thoughts of romance swept from my mind. "He knows about 'The Star-Spangled Banner'! How did he find out? I haven't said a word. Did you say anything? No, of course, you wouldn't say anything. And I'm sure P.J. and Chris wouldn't say anything."

"Mr. H. talked to the people at the music store. It isn't every day that they sell forty copies of a song about a bullfrog. They gave him a description of Dooley."

"Oh, no! What did Dooley say?"

Rachel shrugged. "That he had an evil twin. What else could he say?"

"What's going to happen now?"

"Nothing. Mr. Hawkins just narrowed his eyes in this kind of life-threatening way and told Dooley he was going to be watching him."

I shivered. "I'm surprised he got off that light."

"Yes, but Mr. H. didn't have any real evidence."

"What about the description of Dooley?"

"Mostly bluff," Rachel said. "The thing is there have to be lots of olive-skinned guys who have dark sleepy eyes and a sinister expression."

"Oh, heaps of them," I said in a faint voice.

"Anyway, Mr. Hawkins isn't ready to make an issue

of it. He's too busy cracking down on the battery-throwing ring. The latest is he found some batteries in the janitor's broom closet. The janitor claims he only picked them up in the hall, but now Hawkins is getting thoroughly weird about it. He's started to wonder who he can trust, if anyone."

"How do you find out these things?"

"I have my sources." Rachel examined her nails. "Actually, my mother knows Mrs. Hawkins, but don't spread it around."

"How is Dooley taking getting caught?"

"Okay." She smiled. "Actually, it's all a part of his plan."

"Don't tell me about it." I covered my ears.

"I told you it wasn't anything illegal. What's got into you, Andie?"

"I don't know," I admitted. "My nerves aren't what they used to be."

"Pete getting to you, huh?"

"No! That's not it! What is this everybody keeps giving me about Pete? Unlike some people I can name, I am *ready* for a mature involvement."

"What are you talking about?" She looked at me in surprise. "I'm not giving you a hard time."

"Well, Chris has been."

"Oh, Chris. He would."

"Chris just doesn't seem to believe that people can care about each other so much that they want to be with each other all the time. He can't seem to grasp that some people like the kind of secure, committed relationship that I have with Pete."

"Don't look at me. I'm all in favor of you and Pete having a secure, committed relationship."

"Hold on to that thought, Rache." I smiled. "Pete thinks he and I should eat together every day. Any time I want to see you, he says, you can come eat lunch at our table."

"What!" she screeched. "The nerve!"

I made a fast getaway.

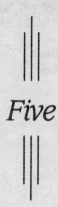

Five

Mom couldn't seem to understand that once-a-week grocery shopping just wasn't enough with P.J. and his friends making daily forays on the provisions. Not that she was a slow learner, but the following Monday morning when I opened the refrigerator, there was no milk. Also there were no eggs. And when I checked the freezer, the bagels were gone too. I shook a box of cornflakes. What would they taste like with orange juice poured over them, I wondered.

P.J. sat at the counter taking the last few bites of a toasted bagel with cream cheese.

"P.J.!" I said in a dangerous voice. "Did you eat every last thing in the house?"

He hastily pulled on his parka. "I think there are some cornflakes in there somewhere. I've got to go, Andie." He gulped down the rest of his glass of orange juice.

"Hey, you can't go yet! I haven't even gotten dressed!"

"Don't worry about that. I've fixed it for Chris to pick you up. He's got his Mom's car. I've got to get Susie to school early for a drama club audition today." The kitchen door slammed behind him.

"Mom!" I wailed.

My mother came trailing down the stairs in a rose-colored peignoir. Her auburn hair tumbled around her face, and she looked lovely. But right at that moment I would have happily traded her for one of those earnest-looking mothers on television commercials who keep obsessing about whether their families are getting enough vitamins. In my opinion there wasn't currently enough concern in this household about whether I got enough vitamins. Or even enough food.

"There is nothing to eat in this house!" I cried.

"Don't be silly, Andie. There has to be something to eat." She opened the fridge. "Hmm. I didn't realize we were out of milk."

"We are out of everything."

"You could have a nice slice of cheese and an apple maybe." She pulled out a tiny square of cheddar that would have been enough, maybe, for an adolescent mouse.

"You must be kidding!" I said.

"Okay, calm down." Mom reached for her pocketbook. "Why don't you and P.J. just drop by one of those fast-food places and get yourself something?"

I explained that P.J. had already left for school, after eating the last bagel, and that I was catching a ride with Chris.

"Chris won't mind running you by some place to eat, I'm sure. It won't take more than a minute."

"Have you thought about what you're going to have for breakfast?" I asked. "And what about Richard? Have you thought about him?"

"Richard left early," she said serenely. "He's going to a power breakfast, whatever that is. And as for me, an apple will be fine."

There was one thing about Mom's using apples for inspiration. Kept in her desk drawer, they did offer a sort of famine insurance.

As it turned out, Chris was happy to take me by a fast-food place. "Maybe I'll get something myself," he said. "I didn't have that much to eat for breakfast. My little brother's gerbil got lost, and things got kind of hectic at our place for a while."

The windshield wipers clacked monotonously as we pulled into the drive-through lane. It was a wet morning and the windows kept misting up. Three cars were ahead of us in line and everyone's headlights were turned on.

"Hey, look!" said Chris. "There's Dooley."

I turned around and saw Dooley scrambling out of his Jeep.

"Yo, Dooley!" yelled Chris.

Dooley walked with long steps toward the entrance and the glass door closed behind him.

Chris looked puzzled. "I guess he didn't hear me."

"What does he want to eat breakfast here for?" I asked. "Rachel told me Dooley's dad's girlfriend was giving him scrambled eggs every morning whether he wanted them or not."

"Maybe he's afraid she's dosing them with arsenic."

The cars in our line inched slowly forward. The fast-food place had a new streamlined procedure—you paid at one window and picked up at another. It seemed to have slowed their service by half. "Don't worry," Chris assured me a few minutes later. "We've got lots of time. No problem." The car ahead of us inched forward.

"There's Dooley. He's come out." I rolled down my window. "Dooley!" I called.

Dooley's Jeep backed out and drove right past us, a plume of exhaust spouting from its rear. Chris beeped, but Dooley didn't look around.

Chris frowned. "I wonder why he changed his clothes."

"He changed his clothes?"

"Sure. Didn't you see? When he went in, he was in black jeans and a leather jacket, and when he came out, he was wearing those old ripped Levi's and that red T-shirt he washes the car with."

"May I take your order please?" asked the electronic voice of the speaker.

"Yeah, uh—what do you want, Andie?"

I ordered a Danish and milk. Chris got a sausage biscuit and coffee. Once we got our food unwrapped and started eating, we pulled out onto the highway.

"Why would Dooley go in there to change his clothes?" I asked. "It doesn't make sense."

"Nothing makes any sense," said Chris. "I tell you, Andie, if I were the type who let things get to me, I could get really down about all this. I used to have two good friends. Now what have I got?"

I bit into my Danish. "Now you've just got me."

"Yeah."

"You don't have to look so depressed about it. Dooley and P.J. will start coming around once they break up with their girlfriends."

"What's your proof of that?"

"What?"

"I said, what's your proof? What makes you think this isn't the shape of things to come? Maybe everybody in the world is going to pair off permanently. Maybe you hit the nail on the head with that Noah's ark theory of yours." Chris brooded on the slick road ahead of us. "Heck, I've never let a girl come between me and my friends. Never!"

"Oh, I don't know about that."

"Never for long, anyway. But P.J. and Dooley are acting like they've gotten married!"

"Chris, I promise you, you're overreacting."

"I hope you're right."

A pale sheen lay over everything in sight. The pavement of the school parking lot was shiny with damp. Yellow glowed at the windows of the buildings where teachers had turned on the lights. Overhead the sun was only a brighter smudge of fog.

"December," said Chris in disgust. "You can have it."

I had to admit there was a kind of *Hound of the Baskervilles* quality about the scene around us.

When I got inside the building, the dampness still clung to me. People's sneakers had left snail-like tracks and bits of crumpled leaves all over the floor. I opened my locker door gingerly to avoid making any abrupt clattering noise. "The South will rise again!" someone yelled in my ear.

"Eeek!" My own voice was shrill in my ears as my

books slid to the floor. A troll in a Confederate flag shirt slunk off. You only had to look at his snaggle-toothed smirk to see that he had gotten a sick thrill out of scaring me to death. I suppose making me drop my books was the high point of his day.

I picked up my algebra book, holding on to it firmly, in case I needed a weapon, and followed him over to the corner where he was lurking. A bandanna was tied around one of the grease-stained knees of his jeans, and his shirt was halfway unbuttoned. He looked like a quality-control reject from a motorcycle gang, but I was so angry it never occurred to me to be afraid. "Don't you ever do that to me again!" I screamed.

"Who's gonna stop me?" he snarled. "*You*, little girl?"

"Watch it, Wayne." A tall guy hoisted his books out of his locker. "That's Pete Joyner's girl."

I stared at the tall guy, speechless with rage. As if I couldn't stand up for myself! I was no sissy. I could call the police and scream for help as well as the next guy.

"Some people can't take a joke," muttered the troll as he slunk out of the locker alcove.

"What a turd!" a girl in a letter sweater said.

"He's looking for a fight," said the guy next to her. "You've just got to ignore him."

I guessed I should have ignored him. That's what people are always telling you to do with bullies. The problem was I was jumpy. Maybe it was the fog. The fact was, I was in no mood to have strange people jumping at me.

"I didn't know you were Pete's girlfriend," said a girl near me. She had neatly curled hair and a small smile so stiff that it looked as if she had accidentally zapped it with hairspray. She was in my algebra class. Her name was Suzanne Yelverton.

"I thought I saw you drive up with Chris Hamilton," she went on when I didn't say anything. She was still smiling.

"Chris is just a friend," I said. She looked impressed. I guess she figured I had all kinds of boys on the string. But why was I explaining myself to this girl? I didn't even know her. Feeling slightly embarrassed, I turned away and hurried off to my homeroom.

Later, at lunchtime, I looked for Rachel and Dooley. Maybe it was the way I had gotten pegged as "Pete Joyner's girl" at the lockers that morning, but I felt an impulse to assert my independence. I figured I'd eat lunch with Rachel and Dooley instead of with Pete. Unfortunately, I didn't see them anywhere.

"Hey, Andie!" Pete's voice made me jump. "How come you didn't wait for me?"

"I was looking for Rachel and Dooley," I said.

He put his arm around my shoulder and smiled down at me. "I saw them on A wing when I came in. I expect they're going to eat under the stairs. You're the one who told me they sometimes do that, right?"

"Oh. Yeah. They do."

He grinned. "I guess we could go keep them company, if you want. Only it might be a little crowded under there."

"No, no, that's all right. If they're going to eat under the stairs, I guess they want to be alone."

"Sit down and save me a place, huh? I've got to go through the lunch line."

I found an empty table, sat down, and opened my

milk carton. After all, it was no big deal. I could see Rachel anytime.

A minute later Chris slid into the chair beside me. "I've figured it out," he said. "Dooley must be changing into those old clothes because he's hoping his teachers will report him to social services as a neglected kid, or something. What do you think?"

"I think you're out of your mind," I said. "Look at that guy who hangs out at the lockers yelling, 'The South will rise again!' He looks like he crawled out from under a rock, and nobody's turned him in. Believe me, no teacher is going to get all excited about Dooley wearing old clothes." I speared a limp green bean with my fork.

"I guess you're right." Chris looked disappointed. "Betcha Dooley hasn't thought of that, though. The poor guy is grasping at straws." He reached for his pat of butter.

"Hey, you can't eat here."

"Why not?"

"Because Pete told me to save a place for him."

"That's okay. I don't mind if he eats with us. There's plenty of room."

I thought about it. "Of course, he *did* say I could have my friends eat with us."

Chris looked at me with pity. "You are so far gone," he said. "I'm not kidding you, Andie. Next thing you know he'll be blowing your nose for you."

"Look, I don't tell you how to live your life, do I?"

"Okay, I won't say a word. Be his love-slave. Have it your way."

"Do you have to be so gross?"

"I'm only trying to help. But believe me, this is the

thin end of the wedge. Start letting them tell you what to do and it just gets worse."

"I appreciate your concern." Unfortunately, Chris did not seem to recognize the heavy sarcasm.

"Well, all right, then," he said.

"So, how are things with Fiona?" I asked pointedly. He'd love it if I started telling him how to behave with Fiona, I thought.

"We're going out Friday night." Chris buttered his roll. "But she acted kind of suspicious of me like she wondered if I had some hidden motive in asking her out. Why do people have to be that way? Why can't people just go out and have a good time and let that be the end of it?"

"With you, Chris, that *is* the end of it."

"You know what I mean. People are so *sticky.* It's this I-belong-to-you-you-belong-to-me stuff. I saw a guy and girl this morning, and they were wearing matching I.D. bracelets."

"I've seen that. That's not so strange."

"I'm not finished. And he had his hand in the pocket of her jeans and she had her hand in the pocket of his jeans."

"They sound very close."

"Close? They were a traffic hazard. They tripped coming up the front steps, and I thought they were going to land on their faces and end up having his-and-her plastic surgery."

I became conscious that Pete was looming over us.

"Hi, there, Hamilton." Pete's face was carefully expressionless.

"Chris is going to eat with us," I explained.

"That's good," Pete said. He put his tray down on the table and lowered himself into a chair with his usual care. I could tell he was not happy about Chris eating with us, but the question was, how unhappy was he? I searched his face. He looked the same as always, the dark eyebrows, the slight space between his front teeth, the kind brown eyes. Except they didn't look so kind right at that moment.

A battery fell onto Pete's plate. He frowned at it, then picked it up with his thumb and forefinger and laid it down on the table.

I heard a clatter behind me. Another falling battery. I had to quell the impulse to cover my head with my tray.

Pete surveyed the cafeteria suspiciously. "Somebody's throwing batteries."

"He's quick on the uptake too," Chris said admiringly.

Pete paid no attention to him, fortunately.

A tray crashed at the back of the cafeteria, and I wheeled around in my seat.

"My God! Look, Andie! It's Dooley!" cried Chris.

The tableau I saw at the back of the cafeteria seemed like a moment frozen in time. Dooley stood in front of Wayne Tyler, his finger resting on Wayne's greasy Confederate flag shirt. Then, almost in slow motion, Dooley drew back his fist and socked Wayne in the jaw.

"Je-rusalem!" cried Chris, jumping to his feet.

All over the cafeteria, chairs were scraping against the floor as people scurried to get a better view. "Fight!" someone yelled.

I grabbed Chris's shirttail. "Don't get involved, Chris. I don't want every single person I know to get expelled."

"It's that Wayne Tyler," said Pete. "He's always getting in fights."

The blow Dooley had delivered had sent Tyler reeling, but I saw the flash of his teeth as he came back grinning and socked Dooley in the stomach. Dooley buckled.

"Pete!" I cried. "Can't you separate them or something?"

"And get expelled right along with them?" he asked. "No, thanks."

I noticed resentfully that the lunchroom personnel had come out to get a better view and a teacher stood with folded arms in a nearby corner. True, she was a small teacher, but she might have tried to exert a little moral authority, at least.

Rachel came up behind Tyler with a tray, closed her eyes tight, and brought the tray down on his head. He grunted, then quickly turned around. I jumped to my feet. I couldn't very well let him murder Rachel. We weren't that far away from the fight, but a big circle had formed around the participants, and it was getting to the point that we couldn't see what was happening.

"Where are you going, Andie?" Pete asked.

"Rachel's in there somewhere," I said. "I've got to help her."

"You'd better stay out of it," said Pete.

I shook off his hand.

"Oh, okay. Have it your way," Pete clenched his teeth. "If you're set on it, then I'm coming too."

The crowd encircling the fight parted to let Pete through. "Come on," he said. "Break it up."

It was not a fight according to the Marquess of Queensberry's rules. It was more like a scene out of mud wrestling. Dooley was down on the floor but had grabbed hold of Tyler's foot and wouldn't let go.

"Come on, you guys," Pete said. He grabbed Tyler's shoulder. Seizing his opportunity, Dooley gave a mighty tug on Tyler's leg. Tyler went down on top of Dooley, and the two of them lay there pummeling each other and grunting.

"Give me a hand, Chris," Pete said. "I'll get the guy on top. You sit on MacKenzie."

"No way," said Chris. "Dooley'd never let me forget it if I tried something like that."

Rachel was gnawing anxiously on her knuckles, but I was relieved to see that she didn't have a black eye. Whatever had happened, Wayne hadn't actually hit her.

Pete pulled Tyler up off Dooley. Dooley struggled to his feet and tried to get at Tyler again, but a couple of other guys held his arms.

"Leave me alone," Dooley protested. "I'm not doing anything. Just let me at that guy, that's all."

Suzanne Yelverton's eyes were glittering. I think she hoped for more violence.

The teacher came over. "Back to your tables, everybody," she said. "You boys know what this means. To the office—and I mean now."

"Dooley threw the first punch," put in Suzanne eagerly.

I caught Rachel's eye. She must have wondered if Suzanne had seen her hit Wayne with the tray and was going to snitch about that too.

"Well, Wayne threw a battery at Dooley," Rachel retorted. "It landed right in his banana pudding."

"I don't care who did what," the teacher said. "Off to the office."

When the teacher collared Dooley and Wayne, Dooley was wiping his mouth with his sleeve. His lip was still bleeding as the teacher marched them out of the cafeteria.

"I don't understand why people do these things," Suzanne said primly. "They know they're going to get suspended."

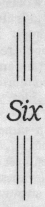

Six

I was copying down my algebra assignment from the board when I noticed that Miss Dew was filling out a form at her desk. When I went up to sharpen my pencil, I saw Dooley's name had been written in at the top of the page. Under his name was a half page of blank lines titled "Observations." I guessed that the fight in the cafeteria had prompted the appearance of this form because, in general, all anyone could observe about Dooley was that he took a lot of naps.

The intercom over the blackboard filled the classroom with an empty roar. Then an electric crackle spit the ominous words, "Andrea Baker to the office, please." I looked at Miss Dew in alarm.

"Take your books, Andie," said Miss Dew. "You might not get back by the end of the period."

I searched my mind hastily, but couldn't think of anything I had done that was criminal.

When I got to the administration building, I saw Pete in the waiting area outside Mr. Hawkins's office with a couple of other kids. Two chairs on either side of Pete had been left empty. People instinctively felt he needed plenty of elbow room. I sat down next to him. He smiled and let his arm fall along the back of my chair, which was comforting.

"Do you have any idea what this is about?" I whispered.

"They always call in witnesses when they have a fight. Don't worry about it."

"I always worry when I get called to the principal's office. Why do they call witnesses if all they're going to do is expel everybody anyway?"

"I guess it's called due process."

Chris came in next and sat down next to me.

"Are you a witness too?" I asked him.

"I'm an innocent bystander," he said. "That's my story and I'm sticking to it."

Mr. Hawkins put his head out of his office. "Elwood Joyner," he said.

Pete flushed and rose from his seat.

"Elwood?" said Chris as soon as Pete had shut the door of the office behind him. "What kind of name is that?"

"It's his grandfather's name." Pete's first name was one of the burdens of his life. He went by his middle name, but Elwood kept popping up on school records.

"Do you really like that guy, Andie?"

I stiffened. "You aren't going to say anything nasty, are you, Chris? Because apart from the obvious fact that you might hurt my feelings, I would like to point out that Pete could be coming out that door any minute and he might just flatten you."

He folded his arms. "Since you put it that way, I'm not going to say anything nasty."

We sat in silence for a minute.

"Excuse me for saying it," I said, "but you seem to be in an awfully bad mood lately."

"I'm fine."

"That's good." I looked at him uneasily. I knew it was tough on Chris the way that P.J. and Dooley were always off with their girls these days, but it wasn't as if Chris couldn't be off with a girl himself. Girls were constantly chasing him. I felt extremely fortunate that P.J. had warned me about Chris in time to prevent my getting a crush on him, because getting a crush on Chris was something that could happen to absolutely anybody. Look at Rachel. It had happened to her, and she was a very intelligent person.

"You need to get yourself a new girl, Chris," I said kindly. "That always cheers you up."

Pete came out of Mr. Hawkins's office and gave me the thumbs-up sign. I motioned him to come over to me. "What did he ask you?" I whispered.

"He's real interested in Wayne Tyler." Pete shrugged. "Don't ask me why."

"Probably wants to ask him for a date," said Chris.

"Andrea Baker," called Mr. Hawkins from his door.

I jumped a mile. I had to just keep telling myself that I hadn't done anything wrong. My problem was that just being in the principal's office made me feel queasy.

"Have a seat," said Mr. Hawkins as I walked into his office. He shuffled a stack of papers on his desk. I noticed his eyes looked like steel ball bearings. "I understand you were present during the disturbance today in the cafeteria. Just tell me in your own words what happened."

"I was just an innocent bystander," I whispered.

"I'm not accusing you of being in the fight," he said. "Just tell me what happened."

"I couldn't really see anything. All I saw was Pete pulling two guys apart." I thought it best not to let on that I even *knew* Dooley.

I expected to get the third degree. Mr. Hawkins narrowed his eyes, and I felt my stomach shrink painfully. "Do you have any reason to think that Wayne is taking drugs?" he asked me.

My mouth fell open. "I don't even know Wayne. I mean, I've just seen him around."

"The way that he, uh, dresses," said Mr. Hawkins, narrowing his eyes. "Does this have to do with some kind of cult, as far as you know? You've never heard him speak of 'sacrifices'?"

Personally, I doubted Wayne even knew a word as long as *sacrifices* but I just mutely shook my head.

What amazed me was that Mr. Hawkins didn't seem to be particularly interested in the cafeteria fight. He was absolutely fixated on Wayne, and it sounded as if he thought Wayne was involved in all sorts of dreadful activities like Satan worship. That was what you had to expect if you dressed and acted like a degenerate, I decided. Somebody was going to believe you were one. Come to think of it, Wayne *could* be into Satan worship for all I knew. I was only glad when I finally convinced Mr. H. that I didn't know the guy. I wasn't able to start breathing properly again until I got out of his office.

* * *

After school Chris didn't ride home with P.J. and me, but he stopped by our house anyway. "Hawkins is flipping out," Chris announced as soon as he threw open the kitchen door.

"You're right about that," I said, remembering the peculiar questions Mr. H. had asked me. I rummaged around in the back of a cabinet and came up with some crackers.

"That probably explains why Dooley only got two days of in-school!" Chris said.

"No joke!" said P.J. "Is that all he got? And you know that Suzanne Yelverton was going all over the place telling people Dooley threw the first punch too. Dooley's got the magic touch. It's the only explanation."

I, too, was amazed Dooley had gotten off so lightly. "What about Wayne?" I asked. "What happened to him?"

"He probably won't be able to come back to school in this century," said Chris.

"Why? Why were they so tough on Wayne and so easy on Dooley?"

"I happen to have the story on that." Chris lowered his voice. "Old Wayne looked so weird that Hawkins had absolutely convinced himself that Wayne had listened to rock music until he was brainwashed into devil worship."

P.J. laughed. "Hawkins is unbelievable. Where does he get this stuff?"

"Yeah, but he got the cops in to search Wayne's locker, and guess what they found?"

"A voodoo doll with Mr. H.'s name on it?"

"No, stupid. Batteries. Wayne had about six pounds

of batteries in there. Turns out he sweeps the floors at Radio Shack, and he'd been stockpiling dead batteries."

"Wayne was the mastermind of the battery war?" I exclaimed. "You're kidding me!"

"Maybe not the mastermind," Chris said. "But when other people with more sense dropped out of it, Wayne was still going strong. That's what started that fight with Dooley, you know. Wayne threw a battery at him."

"Wayne was just looking for a fight," said P.J.

"So was Dooley," I put in.

They both looked at me. "I'm just stating the obvious," I said. "I mean, Pete got a battery thrown at him too, and he didn't go up and sock Wayne."

P.J. snorted. "Yeah, but if Pete went after Tyler, that wouldn't be a fight. It'd be murder."

"It's just that Pete is too sensible to get mixed up in a dumb fight," I said.

"Don't pay any attention to her," said Chris. "It's temporary insanity."

I sighed. I was pretty used to the guys being down on Pete. It was a strange kind of possessiveness. They didn't look at me in a romantic way themselves, but they didn't want me to be involved with anybody else. "I guess Dooley is pretty happy about getting off so light," I said.

"Not that you'd notice," Chris said. "I saw him sixth period, and he looked awfully low."

"In-school suspension is no picnic," said P.J. "You're in with all those kids with tattoos. You have to eat with them at a special table in the cafeteria and never say a word all day. I'd hate it."

"It's not as much fun as eating with Susie," Chris said. "That's for sure. By the way where is Susie-Q?"

"She's having all her wisdom teeth out."

"How about that!" Chris brightened. "The poor kid'll be out of commission for a week at least. Maybe even longer."

"Yeah. You'd think she'd have waited until Christmas break to get it done. What am I supposed to do while she's in the hospital?"

Chris looked at the ceiling and said nothing, which I thought was tactful of him, considering his strong views on coupledom.

P.J. jumped up. "How about we go shoot some baskets?"

Chris grinned. "I think I could fit you into my busy schedule."

They grabbed their jackets and headed for the door. Chris paused a moment, no doubt remembering all the time I had spent holding his hand while P.J. was off making out with Susie Skinner. "Want to come along, Andie?"

"Gee, thanks, I'd *love* to shoot baskets." I glanced up at the clock. "But I have to stand by for Pete's four-thirty phone call."

"Sure you do," said Chris. "Of course you do. We understand." He closed the door quietly behind him.

The boys hadn't been gone long before Rachel came over. "Talk fast," I told her. "Pete calls at four-thirty."

She threw herself down on the family room sofa. "I don't know how much longer Dooley can take this, Andie."

"Take what? He got off light. All Mr. Hawkins seemed to be interested in was Wayne."

"Yeah," said Rachel.

I couldn't understand why she didn't seem happy. "Of course, maybe the other shoe hasn't dropped yet," I said. "Maybe Mr. Hawkins is just gathering his energy for the big pounce. I happened to see that Miss Dew was filling out a form on Dooley this morning."

Rachel perked up. "Tell me more! What did the form say?"

"I'm not sure. Something about observation."

"Ah! They've sent out the observation forms."

Sometimes I felt as if I were in a foreign country. Almost four months at Westmarket High and I still hadn't learned all the ins and outs of the system. "What's an observation form?"

"Like if a teacher thinks some kid is acting strange, she turns in a slip to the office. Then the office sends out forms to all of the kid's teachers asking them if they've noticed anything wrong. If everybody agrees the kid's got a problem, they call the parents in for counseling."

"Dooley doesn't exactly act strange, though," I said. "Mostly, in school, he just doesn't pay much attention."

"Come on, Andie. You were the one who was saying he was acting weird. Remember? After he switched the band music?"

"You think that's what brought this on?"

"And then there was the cafeteria fight."

"You think they're going to call Dooley's dad in?"

"Maybe. That's what Dooley's hoping. His dad would hate that. Dooley's dad is awfully concerned about how things look. Especially now that he's in this new job. He's very insecure."

I could see that Dooley was not the ideal kid for an insecure parent who was concerned about appearances.

"And let me tell you what Dooley—"

The ring of the phone interrupted Rachel. "That's Pete," I said.

"Excuse me for interrupting you," said Rachel politely. "I'll catch you at a more convenient time."

I shrugged as I picked up the phone. Everybody was so difficult lately. Rachel knew that Pete always called at four-thirty. She didn't have to flip out about it. I heard the door slam behind her.

As soon as I heard Pete's voice on the line, I knew something was the matter.

"What's wrong?" I asked.

"Somebody asked me where things stood with you and Chris today."

"We're just friends!" I cried. "Anybody could tell them that."

"The trouble is, Andie, nobody believes that anybody can just be friends with Chris. He's got a reputation." He hesitated. "I'm not sure I believe it myself."

"Oh, good grief!"

"What's that supposed to mean?"

"Why does everybody have to be so touchy?" I wailed.

"I can't help it. When I see you with Chris, I get this feeling I'd like to bash his head."

"Control it," I said, alarmed. "You definitely have to control that impulse."

"Of course I'm not going to bash his head," Pete said patiently. "I'm not that kind of guy. You know that. Besides, do you think I want to get sent to Outer Mongolia permanently, like Wayne Tyler?"

"What happened to Wayne Tyler, anyway?"

"I don't know what happened to him, Andie. I don't care. I thought we were talking about us."

I swallowed. "I think you'd better come over. We can talk better then."

Pete picked me up in one of his family's roomy cars. Since his mother was five feet eleven inches and his father was six feet five inches, all of the Joyners' cars were built on generous lines. You could have played Ping-Pong on the hood of any one of them.

"I'm glad you asked me to come over," he said. "Because when we're together, I always feel a whole lot better."

"Me too." I was getting that warm, tingly feeling. Pete's brown eyes did that to me. Then I realized I shouldn't be seeing his eyes. "Watch the road!" I yelped.

He looked surprised.

"I'm sorry," I explained, "but I guess I am unusually sensitive to issues of road safety."

Pete pulled the car off the road.

"What are you doing?" I asked.

"Being sensitive to issues of road safety." He pulled me close and kissed me softly.

I gave a happy sigh. "This is better than fighting, isn't it?"

"I didn't know we were fighting."

"I just mean all that stuff about Chris. Who cares what other people think about me and Chris? You can't let other people tell you who your friends are going to be, can you?"

"I guess not." He kissed me again.

It might not be love or a mature and lasting relationship, I thought, but whatever it was, it sure was nice.

Seven

Days went by, a few early Christmas cards came. At school Dooley continued to lead a charmed life. Nobody called him to the office. Nobody expelled him. He served his two days of in-school suspension and that was it.

Snow and sleet began to fall on a Thursday afternoon, so school let out early. Icy weather doesn't come often in our part of North Carolina, and when it does, everything shuts down. People stay glued to the radio and TV watching to see what's closed. Generally, the answer is—everything.

The doorbell rang. To my surprise I found Dooley at the front door. "Is Rachel here?" he asked.

"No, she's not. Come in." I pulled him inside. Flecks of ice clung to his parka.

"Rachel's not at home," he said disconsolately.

"Nobody's over there." He came in to the family room and flopped down in a chair, but he didn't touch the towel I dropped in his lap.

"Dry off, Dooley! You're going to catch pneumonia."

"Not a chance, man. Pneumonia? No such luck. Heck, I can't even get arrested."

It certainly wasn't for lack of trying, I thought. I grabbed the towel and started drying his hair.

"What are you doing?" he protested. "Stop that!"

"What you need is some hot cocoa. P.J. is upstairs. Do you want to go up there? I could bring your cocoa up." I backed away from him, watching his face anxiously. The lids of his eyes looked heavy, and the long, thin line of his mouth was turned down at the ends. He looked extremely depressed. "Or I'll get P.J. to come on down."

"I'm not in the mood for any of P.J.'s jokes."

"I'll tell him not to make any jokes."

"Look, I gotta go."

"Wait a minute. I'll do the hot chocolate in the microwave. It'll just take a second."

"Don't bother." He stood up and ran his fingers through his hair. "I'm out of here."

"Don't go, Dooley!" I cried. "It's so yucky out there."

He hesitated. "Andie, did you ever try to fix something and no matter what you did it didn't seem to help any?"

I couldn't come up with any examples from my own life that would be helpful. I had never tried beating my head against a brick wall the way Dooley was doing.

P.J. came thundering down the stairs and burst into

the family room. "Dooley, man, am I glad to see you! I saw the Jeep outside. Susie's got all her wisdom teeth pulled, and all she does now is sit on the couch with a couple of ice packs. Can you believe that? She's not exactly a bundle of laughs, let me tell you."

"I know just how she feels," muttered Dooley.

"I know what! I'll call Chris!" P.J. was so pleased to see Dooley, he seemed completely unaware that Dooley wasn't exactly bubbling over with *joie de vivre*. "Hey, you've got four-wheel drive. How's about we go cruising and pull out the poor suckers who get themselves stuck in ditches?"

Dooley thrust his hands in his pockets. "Okay," he said in a colorless voice.

"Great! This'll be great. Got a chain? Don't worry. Chris probably has a chain."

P.J. was still talking about chains and four-wheel drive and sandbags as they left. He wasn't the world's most sensitive person.

Mom trailed downstairs. "Was that Dooley?" I nodded. "What brought him over? He hasn't been around for ages."

I was surprised she had noticed. She opened the refrigerator and peered inside. "I haven't had to buy quite as many groceries lately," she remarked, "since the boys haven't been coming by every day after school." She stared at the open refrigerator. "If we get snowed in for several days, I wonder if we'll have enough to eat. Maybe I'd better ask Richard to bring home some milk."

I had an impulse to slap a gold star on her forehead—I was happy to see that she had developed an interest in laying in provisions. I am not deeply into food, but I had been forced to reflect lately that a certain bare minimum is necessary to sustain life.

"Are we really supposed to be snowed in for days?" I asked.

"That's not what they're forecasting, but I think it's best to be prepared for the worst."

I was to remember her words in the days ahead.

"Maybe I'll go out and get the mail," my mom said. "After all, if I wait it's only going to get nastier." She fetched her parka out of the coat closet.

A few minutes later she came back in and shook the ice off her jacket. "Isn't this nice?" she said. "We got a Christmas card from Pete."

"For me?"

"No, it's to Richard and me."

I peered over her shoulder as she took it out of the envelope. The card was a vast, gold-rimmed affair, the sort of thing that's usually sent out by savings and loan institutions. The picture on the front was of a frozen pond with a couple of ducks flying over it.

She opened the card. "Merry Christmas," it said. It was signed, "Your future son-in-law."

"Mom," I said, "Pete's crowding me."

The next day at lunch I didn't mention the Christmas card, but I tried to attack the issue indirectly.

"I really need more time with my friends," I told Pete. "What with my schoolwork and all, I'm so booked up that I hardly have time to breathe."

"What are you saying?" He looked uneasy.

"I don't think we have to talk every single afternoon on the phone, do you?"

"No?"

"No," I said. "I feel so tied down having to be by the phone at four-thirty every afternoon. It's limiting."

"Don't you want to talk to me? I want to talk to you."

"Yes, of course I do. But not every single day."

"No problem. I understand. I'll just call you Mondays, Wednesdays, and Fridays."

I looked at him helplessly. "I just need my own life," I said. "I don't want to be all booked up all the time."

"I didn't know you felt that way." He put his hand over mine. His eyes were clouded.

"But you see what I mean, don't you?"

"You need more time with your friends. You've said that before. I follow you."

I sighed. "Yes. That's it. I need more time."

"No problem. You can see your friends during the week and see me on weekends. Okay?"

Despair trickled into my heart. Somebody like Pete was just too good to throw away. But I was beginning to feel as if I were in one of those buddy movies where the guys get locked together with handcuffs and can't find the key.

Pete lifted my chin with his fingers. "Don't worry, Andie. It's going to be all right. You can see your friends. Okay? I understand what you're telling me."

During algebra class my mind was, needless to say, not on algebra. All I could think about was Pete. Miss Dew had just put a set of formulas on the board. At least, the board was full of formulas and Miss Dew was holding a piece of chalk and I supposed she had put the formulas up there, but somehow the previous few minutes were a complete blank. She scrubbed at the board vigorously with the eraser. "See?" she said. "It's perfectly simple. Now for number twelve—" Her eyes raked the classroom, and my breath caught in my throat. Number twelve? Number twelve what? "On the twelfth day of Christmas my true love gave to me . . ." I desperately tried to gather my scattered thoughts. Miss Dew was going to call on me. I just knew it.

"Dooley," Miss Dew said.

"Whaa?" said Dooley.

I sagged in relief. With Dooley up at the board, I had a few more minutes to figure out what was going on. I leafed frantically through my book. At last I found the right page, and things began to come back into focus for me. Problem number twelve—there it was.

"Would you put number twelve on the board, please?" Miss Dew looked at Dooley and tilted her head with an expression of concern. I guess she had been alerted to his problems by that observation sheet that had been sent around to the teachers. I wondered if calling on him was her idea of a way to be helpful.

Dooley got up and began to walk to the front of the classroom. I noticed that his leather jacket was more than a little beat-up. It looked like a war relic. Maybe Pete had been right about his grooming. Suddenly Dooley dropped into a crouch and wheeled around facing the class. To my astonishment, I saw he had a gun in his hand.

"Dooley?" twittered Miss Dew anxiously. Dooley waved the gun at her, and she flattened herself against the blackboard with a quick intake of breath.

I had this eerie sensation that we were all turning

into a newspaper headline. I sat there with my mouth hanging open, forgetting to breathe. I couldn't believe that Dooley was going to hurt anybody. It wasn't possible. But when I tried to say something, my voice wouldn't work.

"I guess I'm going to have to blow you guys away," Dooley said. His black eyes narrowed and he smiled.

Suzanne Yelverton began sobbing in big whooping noises. Dooley spun around to face her. "And I'm going to start with you," he growled.

Suzanne's eyes rolled up to show the whites and she slumped in her desk.

"Good grief," said Dooley in disgust. "Can you believe that? She's fainted."

Jack Hendley was edging toward the door. Behind me, I heard soft thuds as the kids hit the deck. I would have tried to take cover, too, if my legs hadn't been limp.

Suddenly Dooley squeezed the trigger and a stream of water hit Suzanne square in the face.

She spit, sat up, and shook her head.

"Hey, it's a water pistol," somebody said in a stunned voice.

I stared at Dooley. It was only a water pistol? This was one of those merry little jokes of Dooley's, like switching the band music? My eyes were drawn back to the pistol in Dooley's hand. It was lethal looking, but now that I had calmed down, I could see it was made of a sort of dull black plastic, not steel. That small but important detail had escaped me in the terror of the moment. It was some comfort that it had escaped everyone else as well. All around me kids were scrambling up off the floor, self-consciously dusting off their clothes.

Dooley sauntered back to his desk and plopped down in it, looking pleased with himself. The water pistol fell down onto his desk.

Miss Dew was having a hard time dealing with the new reality. She leaned against the blackboard for a minute, breathing heavily. "That was not funny, Dooley," she gasped. She tottered over to her desk chair. "I think you had better go to the office." She scribbled out a hall pass.

Dooley glanced around the room and laughed. Then he gathered up his books and walked out. He didn't pick up the hall pass, and I very much doubted that he was on his way to the office.

Jeff Carter chuckled nervously.

A couple of boys in the back of the class were turning the water pistol over in their hands.

"Unbelievable," said one of the guys. "Sure fooled me."

Miss Dew cleared her throat. "Well, now, class. Let's get back in our seats. Who can do, uh—let's see." She glanced down at the book. "What number was that we were on?" She looked at us blankly.

I found out later in the day that Dooley had been suspended. One of the school counselors called his father to set up a series of parent-effectiveness sessions. Randi Drake, who was in the office, during seventh period found out all about it. Jungle tom-toms have nothing on the school gossip line for passing on hot information.

"Can you believe it?" said P.J. as we drove home after school. "Everybody in the class thought that water pistol was the real thing. That cow Suzanne fainted." He snickered.

"Wait a minute," I said. "I was there. It wasn't so funny."

"Come on, Andie," said Chris. "You know Dooley. He wouldn't hurt a fly."

"I know that."

"Okay, then."

"It wasn't funny," I said stubbornly. "Let me tell you, when Dooley pulled out that thing and said he was going to waste the whole class, people hit the floor. I expected the police to show up outside with a bullhorn."

"Come on. Dooley would never shoot anybody."

"I know that. But you can't deny he's been acting weird. Totally weird."

"Geez, you people are such wimps," said P.J., but I noticed there wasn't much conviction in his voice.

As soon as we got home, I went over to Rachel's to see how she was taking the latest development. "Is Rachel here?" I asked.

Mrs. Green dusted an imaginary fleck of dust from the banister. "She's studying, but you can go on up, Andie."

I went up and knocked, but Rachel didn't answer. The frame of mind I was in, she was lucky I didn't kick the door in. When I opened the door, I saw she was wearing earphones. She ripped them off as soon as she saw me. "It worked!" she cried. "It worked."

"Huh?" I stared at her blankly. "Run that by me again?"

"Dooley got expelled," she said. "His dad's been called in for those counseling sessions where they tell you you've been a disaster as a parent. It's perfect!"

I sat down on the bed. "Give that to me again, in

words of one syllable, Rache. Dooley's been expelled and that's *perfect?*"

Rachel beamed. "It's all part of his plan."

"You mean you *knew* he was going to pull that phony gun out in algebra class?"

She shrugged. "Sure. Nothing else worked. You have to admit he *tried* everything else. He finally decided to try the gun thing in algebra. Because of Suzanne being there, he figured that would make the whole thing more believable because everybody knew he had a motive to want her dead the way she'd ratted on him." Rachel giggled. "Somebody told me she fainted."

"Rachel," I said in an awful voice. "What about me? What about your best friend? Don't you think you could have given me a teensy little clue that I was not going to be massacred in algebra?"

"I *tried* to tell you," she said. "More than once. But you were too wrapped up in Pete. Don't you remember when you shut me up because he called?"

I considered that this explanation was petty beyond belief, and I would have said so except that I was already feeling that maybe Rachel was right. Maybe I hadn't been the best listener in the world lately.

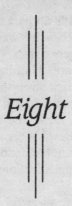

Eight

After Dooley and his dad started the counseling sessions, Dooley was admitted back into school, conditionally. He could keep going as long as he and his dad kept attending the counseling sessions twice a week. Rachel reported that Dooley's dad was extremely bent out of shape. The counselor was half his age and acted as if she didn't realize he was an important executive at Tex-rel. Instead she treated him like a pretty poor excuse for a parent. For the first time in weeks I noticed that Dooley was going around with a smile on his face. Dooley's plan to embarrass his dad had seemed silly to me, but I couldn't argue with success. For once, Dooley was pretty happy.

Monday morning P.J., Chris, and I pulled up in the school parking lot next to Dooley. Dooley leapt out of his Jeep and smacked the hood of our car with his hand. "They're married!" he yelled.

We all opened our doors and jumped out at once. "Calm down, Dooley," said P.J. "Get a grip. What's the matter? What's going on?"

"My dad has *married* that witch. Can you believe it? They came in last night and showed me the marriage license."

"I guess it was the real thing," said Chris dubiously.

"Sure it was the real thing. What do you think?" Dooley groaned. "I thought I had convinced him. I mean, good grief, any idiot could see that everything was fine until she came along. All he had to do was get rid of her, and we'd be back the way we were. Why'd he have to go and do something like this?"

"Maybe they're in love," I offered.

They looked at me as if I were a skunk at a garden party.

"Seems kind of funny that they didn't have a wedding or anything," said P.J. "What do you think? It's kind of strange."

"They were probably afraid Dooley would lob a bomb at the minister," said Chris.

"I'd have tried something," said Dooley. "I can't *believe* this. After everything I did! The forty blinking pieces of frog music—that wasn't cheap, you know. And getting in that fight with Wayne—you should smell that guy close up. Fighting's not my thing, man. You know that. And then those dippy counseling sessions." He clenched his fists. "But I thought it was worth it. I thought I was getting somewhere." He socked the hood.

"Hey, take it easy, man," said P.J. "Don't dent it, okay?"

"He said he had decided to 'regularize his home life.' What is that supposed to mean?"

"He wants you to have a respectable, normal home life," I put in. "He figures you'll straighten out then."

"But the counselor didn't say anything like that," Dooley said. "Honest. It was all stuff about communication and stupid junk like that."

"I guess maybe he came up with the idea on his own," said Chris.

"The witch got to him," Dooley said. "That's all."

"Look, Dooley," I said. "Don't you think you could take all this energy and ambition and imagination and sort of sublimate it into something like getting into a decent college?"

He turned his ripe-olive black eyes on me, and I was forcibly reminded of the day he had pulled out the water pistol. I backed away.

"Just an idea," I said.

"Cheer up, man." Chris slapped Dooley on the back. "This, too, will pass."

"No, it won't," said Dooley. "You don't get it, Chris. They're married."

"They could get a divorce," suggested P.J.

While I fetched my books from the car, the guys started to walk off together. It hit me that I hadn't heard much about Susie Skinner lately. Maybe that romance was fading out. Chris was free as a bird, P.J. seemed to be working his way free from Susie Skinner, and though Dooley was still with Rachel, Rachel wasn't the possessive type. I was the only one who was tied down. Paired off. Trapped. I shifted my books to my hip and started to run to catch up with them, but Pete's voice froze me in my tracks.

A second later Pete appeared beside me and encircled me with his huge arm. "I've got an idea about how you can have more time with your friends and we

can still see each other every day. I could give you a
ride back and forth from school. What about it?"

"I may shoot myself," I muttered.

"What did you say?" He bent down closer to me.

"I don't know, Pete. The problem is that riding
back and forth from school is one of the times I see my
friends."

His brow puckered. "I don't get it. I thought when
you said your friends you meant, like, Rachel and
your girlfriends."

"Yeah, but P.J. and Dooley and Chris are my
friends too."

"Chris." His face darkened. "There he is again."

"And P.J. and Dooley," I added hastily. "Don't
forget about them."

Luckily, at that moment, the bell went off like a
bomb, and I bolted for homeroom.

When I got in from school that afternoon, Mom was
dancing around the living room in black leggings and
an oversize sweatshirt that said "Save the Rain For-
est." She had an old Paul Simon song on the stereo,
"Fifty Ways to Leave Your Lover."

"I got the book in the mail just now!" She snapped
her fingers. "Boy, the relief! It was all stamped and I
went ahead and took it to the post office. Even when I
know it's finished, I just don't feel that *whoosh* of
relief until I get the whole thing completely out of the
house."

It hit me that a book manuscript was like a romance. You had what seemed like a good idea, but you
lived with it on and on and on until suddenly you just
had to get out from under it. And then the relief! I
could just imagine it. The freedom!

From the speaker came the voice of Paul Simon, warbling on in this absurdly carefree way about breaking things off. Mom's record had a scratch on it, and there was a slight blip every six words or so, but it was evident the singer had a very light-hearted attitude about breaking up. I went in the kitchen, poured myself some orange juice, and wished I could feel that way myself.

Pete's family left for Louisiana the day after school let out for the holidays. He had cousins and two sets of grandparents down there, and his family always went for a two-week visit at Christmas. He did send me a dozen red roses that arrived Christmas Eve. The card said, "All my love, Pete."

Over Christmas vacation, Chris broke up with Martha Hemming and took up with Alana Jackson instead. I realized I couldn't remember when I had last heard P.J. mention Susie Skinner. When I was at the mall the day after Christmas returning a sweater, I spotted Susie eating an ice-cream cone. She was with some guy I didn't recognize.

I sat down at the snack plaza with a slice of pizza and my packages.

Chris was coming out of the sports shop when he spotted me. He came over and looked hungrily at my pizza. "Can I have a bite?" he asked.

I pushed it toward him. "Go ahead." I didn't have much appetite lately. I was just going through the motions of eating.

He sat down and bit off the point of the slice, taking the only piece of pepperoni. "I'm thinking of giving up girls for my New Year's resolution," he said, licking his lips.

"That's nice," I said. I had exchanged the pink

sweater Mom had given me for a red one because red was Pete's favorite color. It only occurred to me now that it clashed with my auburn hair.

"Didn't you hear me, Andie? I said I'm thinking of giving up girls."

"I heard you. It sounds like a good idea."

"Maybe I'll get a slice of pizza myself."

A minute later Chris returned with a slice of pizza, sat down, and stretched his long legs out beside the table. "The thing is, I've been thinking about this a lot. Over Christmas Alana called me up and said I was neglecting her. Neglecting her! Like she was a gerbil or something!"

I leaned my chin on my hand because my head felt heavy. "You should have sent her a dozen red roses."

"Are you out of your mind?" He stared at me. "Do you have any idea how much something like that costs?"

"How much?"

"I don't know, but a lot. The thing is, I started thinking, what do I need girls for?"

"Hugging, kissing. In a word, sex."

"You know something, Andie, you're getting kind of fixated on sex."

"No more than you and P.J. and Dooley."

"Yeah, but it's different. You're a girl."

I didn't say anything. Chris's idea of giving up girls sounded good to me. Think of all the trouble you'd save. I had an even better idea—giving up the whole human race. I would become a hermit. I only had to work out a few details about the financing, change of address, things like that. I was feeling pretty low.

Chris looked at me anxiously. "I didn't hurt your feelings by saying that, did I?"

I shook my head.

"What's the matter, then?"

"Chris, how do you break up with somebody?"

"I'd say the easiest way is to let them catch you with another girl." He grinned.

"But what if you don't want another, uh, person? What if what you want is just—freedom?"

"Jeez, Andie, it's no problem. There are hundreds of ways. Like, you say that you think it's time you see other people. That's sort of a code phrase. It means 'Goodbye, sweetheart.' But you'd be surprised at how much better people take it than if you just tell them you're sick of them."

Why was it that nothing Chris said seemed very helpful? Here I was talking to Westmarket High's greatest authority on breaking up, and nothing he said made any sense to me. Was the problem that I was deeply ambivalent? I really, really liked Pete. He made my toes toasty warm just by putting his arms around me. I thought I was going to miss him something fierce. Maybe I didn't want to break up with him after all. Maybe *that* was it. Except that I had this crazy feeling of being trapped.

"I think I want to break up with Pete," I said hoarsely.

"Say no more. You've come to the right guy. Want a list of fifty tried and true exit lines? No, wait a minute. I've got it! What about if you pretend to take up with me? Two birds with one stone. We get rid of Alana and Pete at the same time."

"Certainly not. I have my standards."

"You don't have to get insulting." Chris looked hurt. "Hits you with a sickening thud, huh?"

"It's not that, Chris. Pete is serious about me. I

can't play a trick on him. He asked me how I would feel about living in California. He sent me roses with a card that said "All my love." He sent my mom and Richard a Christmas card signed 'Your future son-in-law.'"

Chris looked appalled. "Jeez, that's terrible. No wonder you want to break up with the guy."

"Actually, it's sweet. But somehow—I don't know how to explain this—it's getting to me."

"You don't have to explain to me, Andie. I'm with you. I understand one hundred percent. Look, I warned you about the guy."

"I've made up my mind," I said suddenly. "I'm going to do it as soon as he gets back from Louisiana."

"I'll drink to that," said Chris.

Chris looked quite pleased. Why didn't I feel pleased, too?

Rachel was having a New Year's Eve party. Her idea was that a party would cheer up Dooley. Mrs. Green was so terrified of Rachel's friends knocking over one of her Chinese vases that the Greens arranged to have the party in the banquet room of the Primrose Inn, a fancy restaurant in town. They were planning to have a seafood buffet and a juice bar. I went with Rachel to pick up her dress from alterations. It was a socko black velvet, cut low in back, with a black and white plaid taffeta skirt. I wasn't sure whether the party was going to cheer Dooley up, but it certainly seemed to be cheering Rachel up.

She came over to my house to look at my dress, a black velvet with bows down the back, more subdued than hers, but with a certain quiet punch.

After we had exhausted the subject of dresses, we

ended up back in the family room. "I hear," said Rachel, "that you're breaking up with Pete."

I was startled. "How did you hear about that?" I was having major second thoughts since I had talked to Chris.

"Dooley told me."

"How did Dooley—Oh, never mind." After all, it was pretty obvious how Dooley had found out. Chris had rented a loudspeaker and spread the news. I flopped down in a chair.

"It's true, isn't it?"

"I don't know."

"Don't get cold feet now, Andie."

I couldn't help it. I had cold feet.

"You can do it at my New Year's Eve party," Rachel offered. "You don't want to do it at school."

I shuddered. "No. That would be awful. There in front of everybody. In fact, I'm not sure I want to do it at all."

"Don't be silly," said Rachel, popping a chocolate in her mouth. "Of course you do." Boxes of chocolates were lying around all over the place since Christmas.

P.J. came in and slammed the kitchen door behind him. "Hey." He grinned. "So, you're going to break up with Pete, huh? Does he know about it yet?"

"She's going to do it at my New Year's Eve party," said Rachel.

"I didn't say that!"

P.J. took a chocolate out of the box.

"The round ones are coconut," advised Rachel.

"It's okay. I like coconut," said P.J. "Buck up, Andie! Have a little backbone!"

"I have plenty of backbone. I'm just not sure I want to break up with Pete!"

"She does," Rachel assured him.

"Look, it's my life, if you don't mind!"

Rachel carefully scrutinized the chocolate in her hand.

"Betcha it's caramel," said P.J.

Rachel bit into it. It was caramel, which slowed her down as it took some time to free her teeth. Finally she said, "Every New Year's Eve party should have an event. This can be our event. You can break up with Pete."

"Yeah," said P.J. "I love it. He'll get real mad and start throwing things around—"

"Hey!" protested Rachel. "Not at my party."

"Pete is not the type to throw things around," I said.

"That's what you think," said P.J. darkly. I began to wonder what his breakup with Susie Skinner had been like. I was getting morbidly curious about everybody's fractured romances lately.

"Anyway," I said. "I'm certainly not going to break up with him at Rachel's New Year's Eve party. When I do it, if I do it, it will be at some quiet time when the two of us are alone. It will be civilized and private. And I wish you all would quit talking about it.

"Hey, I can see it now!" cried P.J. "A flag flying over the school. 'Welcome back, Pete. P.S., Andie is going to break up with you.'"

"Stop it, you two!"

"You had better stop it, P.J. She's really getting mad," said Rachel.

"I'm not doing anything!" P.J. protested.

"Look, Andie," said Rachel. "You have to break up with him soon because everybody knows about it, and pretty soon he's going to hear about it from somebody else, and that would be tacky."

I glared at them. "If certain people would keep their mouths shut, that would be no problem. I just told you, I don't *know* what I'm going to do."

"She's going to break up with him," Rachel told P.J.

"Ooo!" I stomped out of the room.

Pete called me when he got back to town. He wanted to reassure me that he was back in plenty of time for Rachel's New Year's Eve party. I wished I hadn't said anything to Chris about breaking up with Pete. It was going to be awful if everybody kept watching us at the party, waiting for us to break up, when I wasn't even sure I wanted to break up.

Nine

New Year's Eve was rainy and cold. Pete and I had to park our coats with the attendant in the cloakroom and stomp our wet feet on the mat as we went into the party. Mr. and Mrs. Green stood at the door and looked us up and down suspiciously as we came in. Ever since Rachel had gotten into her father's liquor cabinet, thus getting herself almost permanently grounded, the Greens seemed to be perpetually imagining that the typical teenager traveled with a hip flask.

"Next the body search," muttered P.J., who wandered up to us with Alana Jackson. They didn't look particularly lovey-dovey. I noticed Alana was constantly checking out Chris from the corner of her eye. A friend of Pete's collared him and the two of them headed back to the food for the fourth or fifth time.

"I feel sorry for any girl who gets mixed up with

Chris Hamilton," Alana whispered to me. "Personally, I don't think he's capable of caring about anybody."

"He's frivolous," I said. I hardly knew the girl, but she was obviously unhappy about having lost Chris, and it didn't hurt to be agreeable.

She darted a glance in his direction. "He's kind of pathetic, actually. Do you know who that girl is that he's talking to now?"

I shrugged. I was only glad to see there was no sign of Susie Skinner. That would have been one complication too many. I was beginning to see that these recently ended romances could get tricky at parties. I wished I had pointed this out to Rachel when she was making out her guest list.

"Look at her," said Alana spitefully. "She doesn't have any figure at all."

"A very sad case," I agreed. I edged away from Alana as quickly as I could. Actually it had been easy to get away from her because the room was so full of people. I recognized several guys from the football team, and I ended up getting in a long discussion with a couple of band members about whether they should play a practical joke on Dooley just to pay him back. I voted no. I was surprised to find out Rachel knew so many different people. But a good bit later, when I ran into Rachel, she explained. "My parents made me ask all their friends' kids," she said. "Have you ever seen such a bunch of preppie types?"

What I saw was a sea of black dresses. It seemed everybody had had the exact same idea I had of making an elegant, sophisticated, simple statement.

Even with all the people in the room dressed more

or less alike, I had no trouble keeping track of Pete. His head was well above the crowd. I was pleased that he was not sticking by my side the entire time. Maybe his time in Louisiana had been a good thing. It had given us both a little breathing space. I personally was feeling much better. This could be the beginning of a wonderful new year.

"You going to break up with Pete?" P.J. asked me.

"Shut up," I said.

"Pretty sensitive about it, aren't you?"

"I never said I was going to break up with Pete at Rachel's party. I probably won't break up with him at all. Now go away, please." I turned my back on him.

I saw Dooley gnawing on a jumbo shrimp.

"Happy New Year, Dooley." I waved.

He came over to me. "I hear you're going to break up with Pete tonight."

"Would you stop saying that," I hissed. "There's nothing to it. Everything's fine between me and Pete. What would he think if he heard you saying that?"

"He'd think you were breaking up, I guess." Dooley flipped the shrimp tail in a nearby ashtray.

"Well, I'm not breaking up with him." What I needed was a change of subject.

I glanced over at the punch bowl and saw Rachel glowing. I had never seen her looking so happy. But then, why not? With Dooley's home life shot to pieces, he appreciated Rachel more than ever. They seemed to have gotten awfully close.

"You're always going some place with Rachel these days, and we don't see much of you," I said to Dooley. "How are things?"

"Awful."

"What's wrong?"

"She's pregnant," he said gloomily.

I dropped my canapé.

"Hey, you dropped your little thingy," he said. "Aren't you going to pick it up or anything?"

"She's *pregnant?*" I breathed.

"Yeah, grim, isn't it? I can't believe that one of these days we're going to have a little witchette around the house."

I struggled to regain my composure. Forget the canapé. "Your stepmother is pregnant," I said and sighed. "You mean your stepmother."

"Yeah. What'd you think?"

"Never mind what I thought."

"Want me to get you something to eat? Not to get personal or anything, Andie, but you could stand to put on a little weight. I'll bet you can see every one of your ribs."

"My life is not easy," I said grimly. "It's hard for me to get anything decent to eat, and when I do it turns out I don't have much appetite."

"I don't see what you're complaining about. You don't have a little witchette on the way over at your house."

"Oh, cheer up, Dooley. Maybe it'll be a boy."

His face cleared. "Yeah, that wouldn't be so bad. Poor little sucker. Feel sorry for him having the witch for a mother. But maybe I could help him out some, show him the ropes, teach him how to make water balloons, that kind of thing."

Rachel came over to us. "Has Dooley told you the big news?"

"Yes. And how."

"I keep telling Dooley it's really good news. When Terri's busy with a new baby, she won't have nearly as much time to get on his case."

"That makes sense," I agreed.

"And there's always the chance she'll get hit by a truck," said Dooley cheerfully. "She's getting kind of slow on her feet."

"Do you have to say things like that?" I said. "It's creepy."

"I'm just trying to look on the bright side. Don't want to ruin Rache's party by being downbeat."

"I believe," I said, "that some people get very fond of their little half-brothers and sisters."

"Jeez," said Dooley. "You make it sound like she's going to have a whole litter of them!"

"Look, Andie," said Rachel, "we'll leave you alone. I know you must be looking for your chance to break up with Pete."

"What *is* this with you people?" I exclaimed.

"She's not going to break up with Pete," Dooley explained. "They're getting along real good."

"At last," I said, "somebody's catching on."

"Dooley's very sharp," said Rachel proudly.

I saw Alana was over by the seafood. I didn't want to get stuck with her again, so I stood beside a bowl of M&M's and began carefully to pick out the red ones. No green ones. I was already fond of Pete, and I didn't want to get carried away. If I got as wild about him as he seemed to be about me, we could end up eloping or something like that. Probably there was nothing to the idea the green ones had love potion qualities, but I figured it wasn't worth taking the chance.

111

Pete appeared at my side. "Have an M&M," I said, popping a red one in his mouth.

"I ran to get over here before midnight," he said, "because you know what happens then. Everybody kisses everybody, and I want to be sure I'm the one kissing you."

"I'm glad you came over, then."

He put his arm around me. "I'm a civilized person, Andie. You know that." His face darkened. "But I swear if I saw Chris trying to kiss you, I'd deck him."

"Absolutely nothing to worry about," I said hastily. "Chris is way over there and we're here. Besides, Chris is just a friend."

"I know that's what you say, but there's something about him—"

"Ten, nine, eight, seven, six," people were chanting. "Five, four, three, two, one—Happy New Year!"

Pete enveloped me in his arms and gave me a lingering kiss. "I've been waiting for this," he said gruffly. "Hang on."

I glanced nervously over in Chris's direction, but as far as I could tell he was busy kissing every girl in the remote vicinity of the punch bowl and was showing no signs of bolting in my direction.

"Here," said Pete. "I wanted to start the New Year right." He was holding a small blue velvet box.

"But you already gave me a Christmas present," I protested. "The roses!"

"Yeah, but this is something special."

I opened it. A ruby ring, its stone surrounded by tiny diamond brilliants, sat nestled in the satin.

"It was my grandmother's," he explained.

I snapped the box closed in a panic. "Pete, I can't take it."

"Look, I want you to have it. What's the problem? It's insured."

"But it's too valuable. Besides, it's an heirloom." I gulped. "It would look like an engagement ring."

"Is that what's bothering you? Don't worry about it. It's not an engagement ring."

"What is it, then?"

He smiled. "It's sort of a preengagement ring."

I felt as if the earth were opening up. "Pete, there's something I need to tell you."

"What's wrong, Andie?"

"I think we ought to start seeing other people."

"What's that supposed to mean? Who is it you want to start seeing?" His face darkened.

"Nobody. I just mean that I think we ought to break up."

"Is this your New Year's present?" he asked bitterly.

"I'm sorry."

"Look, is it the ring, Andie? Forget the ring."

"I just think—"

"Hey, Happy New Year!" cried Chris. "Don't I get a kiss or anything?"

I closed my eyes. "Go away, Chris."

When I opened them, Pete's jaw was clenched, his fists were clenched, and he was glaring at Chris. It was a bad moment. I knew Rachel wanted an event at her party, but I didn't think she wanted actual blood on the floor. "Maybe you'd like Chris to give you a ride home," Pete said curtly. He turned on his heel and strode out of the room.

"What's with him?" asked Chris. "Jeez, I've heard about jealous, but this is ridiculous."

I sniffled. "We b-broke up."

"Jeez, Andie, don't cry here!" Chris was looking around the room desperately. "People are going to start staring. Je-rusalem, they're going to think I said something to you."

"I c-can't help it."

Chris grabbed my elbow and guided me out of the room. "We'll go to the car. You can cry all you want in the car." We stopped at the cloakroom and claimed my coat. The girl there looked at me curiously, and I was glad to wrap a muffler around my head and bury my nose in it.

We went out to Chris's car and got in out of the cold and drizzle. The lights from the Primrose Inn turned the water drops on the windshield into spangles. Our breath fogged up the windows, and we seemed to be in a private little world far from the party.

"I don't get it," Chris said. "Correct me if I'm wrong, but aren't you the one that broke it off?"

"Yes." I sniffled. "I did."

"And didn't you tell me you were ready to break it off?"

"Yes. But I wasn't sure. But when he tried to give me the ring—"

"A *ring?* Jeez, Andie, you did it in the nick of time. This guy is unbelievable."

"He was always so sweet to me," I sobbed. "Always so nice."

"Would you please stop that blubbering?" Chris handed me his handkerchief, and I blew my nose. "Pull yourself together."

"It's just such a shock. I guess I wasn't very smooth about it. It's just when he brought out that ruby ring that belonged to his grandmother, I panicked."

"I guess so. The guy went completely over the top."

"You don't understand at all, Chris. I'm just sorry about hurting his feelings."

"He'll thank you later," said Chris. "Believe me. Feeling better?"

I looked in the rearview mirror and blotted my eyes with a tissue. "I don't guess you could just take me home."

"The only thing is I brought Shauna Eastman. I guess I could go in and explain to her—"

I blew my nose. "No, it's all right. I'm fine. I'll tell you one thing, though. Never again. You were right. It's a bad idea to get involved like that. Guys start thinking they own you. Then you never get to see your friends, and you're all tied down. And you see what it leads to. A scene!" I shuddered.

"It might work out okay if it were the right person."

"Not a chance." I shook my head. "I've learned my lesson."

"You're just upset. Want to go back inside?"

"I guess so. I sure don't want to stay out here. The last thing I want is for people to think I'm out here making out with you."

"That would be the end of the world?" Chris grinned.

"Okay, laugh. But you can't imagine what it's been like to have Pete saying, 'Justin thinks this.' 'People say that.' I just want to get out from under all that gossip stuff and be a private citizen. Freedom—that's what I want for New Year's." I reached for my pocketbook. "I can catch a ride home with P.J. The party's bound to wind down soon."

"Yeah, I noticed Rachel's parents yawning. How'd you like to have a couple of gargoyles like that at your party?" He opened the door. "You okay now?"

"I'm fine." I scrambled out of the car. When Chris and I went back in the restaurant, some other couples were at the cloakroom gathering up their things. But the party still seemed to be in full swing inside the banquet room. P.J., who loved parties, would probably be the last one to leave.

"Jeez," said Chris, "there's Alana over there."

"She came with P.J."

"Talk about vindictive. This is not a girl you want to have as an enemy. Why'd she have to come with P.J.? I mean, what does that tell you? Just after breaking up with me she's going out with my best friend?"

"That she's still carrying the torch?"

"Get out of here! She's just plain mean, that's what. She's probably trying to figure out some way to get back at me. If you don't mind, Andie, I'm just going to stand here a minute with my back turned to her. Let me know when she moves away from the shrimp and stuff."

"It looks like there isn't much shrimp left, Chris."

"She probably ate it all. Anyway, tell me when she moves." He stuffed a handful of M&M's in his mouth. "Hey, these are those Christmas M&M's, aren't they? Just two colors. It's a lucky thing somebody ate all the red out. I don't like the red ones. They're kind of bitter." He devoured another handful.

"Chris," I said, giggling. "You've eaten all the green M&M's."

"Yeah, so what? The party's almost over anyway."

"So nothing." I grinned. "Uh, Happy New Year."

He kissed me lightly on the lips. "Happy New Year, Andie."

About the Author

JANICE HARRELL decided she wanted to be a writer when she was in the fourth grade. She grew up in Florida and received her master's and doctorate degrees in eighteenth-century English literature from the University of Florida. After teaching college English for a number of years, she began to write full time.

She lives in Rocky Mount, North Carolina, with her husband, a psychologist, and their daughter. Ms. Harrell is a compulsive traveler—some of the countries she has visited are Greece, France, Egypt, Italy, England, and Spain—and she loves taking photographs.

The Linda Stories

Read all about the boys in Linda's life... from her first crush to the ups and downs of a powerful true love.

continued

☐ *My Heart Belongs To That Boy*   70353/$2.95

When Linda and Lenny first get together, it's *wonderful*. This is real love, at last! But then Lenny starts cutting school and flirting with other girls, and the fireworks start! Linda still loves him, but she can't help but wonder…how will they ever get it right?

☐ *All For The Love Of That Boy*   68243/$2.95

After a summer apart, Linda is sure she and Lenny will never break up again. It's great to be back with her old crowd, and back in Lenny's arms again…until her friends start drifting apart, and Lenny pulls his craziest stunt ever. With everything changing so fast, will their love change, too?

☐ *Dedicated To That Boy I Love*   68244/$2.75

By senior year Linda knows it's true—Lenny is the love of her life. Even if he *does* still get into trouble sometimes, Linda is determined to stand by him. But then when Lenny finally finds a way to get his act together for good, Linda's world is turned completely upside down!

☐ *Loving Two Is Hard To Do*   70587/$2.95

Linda doesn't set out to have a summer romance…it just happens. Dave is handsome and smart, and he never gets into trouble like Lenny. Soon Linda is back in the city, though, and so is Lenny. She can't have them both…but how can she ever choose between them?